The Wrong Bus
An Urban Christmas Tale

By

John Noel Hampton

The Wrong Bus

Dedicated to:

Thomas G. Clarke for his encouragement, valued advice, love and prayers. You're the best, Tom.

Special Thanks to:

Katherine Tomlinson for years
of advice and encouragement.
You're one of my special "ANGELS."

Here's a great big THANK YOU to Laura Shinn for her assistance on my road to publication.

Find out more about John's work at:
www.johnnoelhampton.com &
www.myspace.com/JohnNoelHamptonAuthor

Contact John Noel Hampton at:
jnhampton@mindspring.com

Blurb

When Ida, a wealthy older optimist, sets out to complete her Christmas shopping, little does she know the dramatic turn her life will take when she decides to go by bus to save a few dollars and becomes the victim of a brutal assault.

Her luck takes a three-sixty turn when Junior, a young African-American student from the wrong side of town with troubles of his own, comes to her rescue—or does it?

Christmas in Los Angeles can bring out the worst in some, but it can also spin misery into miracles and just maybe restore faith.

Reviews

"*The Wrong Bus* is right in so many ways. The story's message is powerful and refreshing."

Rob Dorfmann
Executive Producer/Director/Writer

"*The Wrong Bus* is a story of unexpected connections, a reminder that families come in all configurations and that love is indeed color-blind. It's a joyous celebration of the true spirit of Christmas."

Katherine Tomlinson
Story Authority

CHAPTER ONE

It was a large house that wanted filling. Its gray exterior and once-white columns, parched and peeling from the hot California sun, begged for a good scraping and a fresh coat of paint. The gutter along the upper roof flopped down, its pinions no longer supporting the weight of the pine needles and stagnant water, giving it the look of an elongated, rusty metal basket, poised to topple at any moment. The lower windows were spotless inside and out, but those on the second story hadn't been washed on the outside for over a year. They could manage the inside, the two old women, but the outside needed attention. For over a year now, it had been just the two of them, and the house wanted more.

The *Guest House For Rent* sign in the window next to the front door went mostly unnoticed, the few possible takers seeing it being overpowered by the general disrepair of the structure. Still, it offered some hope of additional voices, new people, maybe even young people to use and enjoy its vast emptiness.

Ida sighed heavily as she stood in the high grass spotted with weeds staring at the decay. Her withered right hand raised to smooth back the gray hairs that the cold, late-December wind had blown astray. She shivered. Winter had laid its usual modest claim on coastal Los Angeles, but it was enough to chill Ida to the bone. It had happened so fast, the deterioration, she thought. Looking at the houses on both sides of hers and across the street, she suddenly felt embarrassed. They were all stately, traditional homes like hers, but theirs seemed freshly painted and had carefully groomed lawns. They were weed-free and storybook perfect in every way. Old Arthur had only been dead for a year, and yet there it was. The house missed his loving care. She gave it one last look, deciding not to dwell on it.

She could see Madeline, struggling to open one of the bay windows in the living room, giving up and moving on to the next one. She watched as Madeline's Rubenesque figure leaned into the next window. With a moan, the frame released its damp grip on the window, allowing it to open two inches.

"Move it to the left. And twist it right a little." Ida's hand did a little circle in the air.

"Whose left?"

Ida motioned with her hand. She watched as her housekeeper pulled on the lower branches, the tree wobbling as it moved. Ida loved Christmas and wanted everything just right. "Perfect. Now close the window. Letting all the cold in."

Madeline shot a menacing look at Ida and shook her head. "Too close to her pennies," she mumbled to herself as she pulled down on the window with her large black hands. A loud creak signaled the window's cockeyed stop just half an inch short of closing. Fisting one hand, Madeline banged on the frame to free it up, but the window refused to move.

"Don't break the glass!" came Ida's unwanted two cents.

Madeline glared at her once again. "Getting on my nerves," she mumbled. She saw Ida, her small, seemingly frail body moving rapidly across the lawn toward the front door as she applied all her weight to the window, and it finally slid home. She heard the planks of the front porch moan and the front door swing open. "Gonna be one of those days."

Ida stopped two steps inside the living room, seeing the blue spruce and smiling. The pungent scent of balsam bounced off the highly polished wooden floors, erasing the strong smell of last night's liver and onions.

"Prettiest tree we ever had."

"Too big," said Madeline.

"Nonsense, say that every year. Repeating yourself. Got no spirit."

Madeline ignored her, mumbling, "Three or four feet. Put it on the table, but no." to herself as she pushed a large cardboard carton across the floor to the card table with her foot.

"Careful. Don't scratch my floor."

"Not scratching the floor. Who polishes it, anyway? Think I want to scratch it?"

Ida knew she had said too much. She bit her lip and smiled. "You do. I know. You do everything. Couldn't stay in this house without you." True, she thought, so true. She could never stay in a house this large alone. But it wasn't just the upkeep of the interior that she depended on Madeline for so much as her companionship, friendship really.

Ida moved to the Steinway Grand nestled in the corner next to the fireplace and righted one of the many silver framed photos that had toppled sometime in the night. She ran her hand over the keys, staring into another of the frames. Her husband Jack's warm smile beamed out to her, his eyes locking on hers, and she plunked a few random notes.

"Don't go getting your hand cream on the ivory now," Madeline cautioned her. It was a proprietary thing with her, the piano being a gift to her from Ida. Ida couldn't play. She plunked and pecked sometimes, which drove Madeline mad, but she had no ear for music. Ida glanced over her shoulder at Madeline who was fussing with the box. She turned back and smiled to herself, closing the lid and winking at Jack as she moved away.

Madeline removed the lid and lifted out a mass of tinsel wrapped around a piece of cardboard. She untied the bright red strand of yarn that held it all in place and set it on the table. Stray needles from last year's tree trailed across the tabletop. She gathered them together with one hand, sweeping them off the edge into the other. "This is the last year we're gonna use this stuff. Time to buy some new tinsel."

"It looks perfectly good to me."

Madeline rolled her eyes. "It would."

A bottle of chilled champagne wrapped in a towel and two flutes sat on a silver tray in the middle of the coffee table. Ida fiddled with the cork for a few moments before handing the bottle to Madeline. With a twist of her wrist, the resounding pop and accompanying fizz brought a smile to both of their faces, erasing all signs of their earlier conflict over the size of the tree. Madeline poured the lightly amber-colored liquid into the two glasses in short drips, hesitating to allow the foam to settle, while Ida switched on the Christmas album she had selected earlier. The old 78 snapped and crackled, giving forth Nat King Cole's mellow version of _Adeste Fideles_. The two women clinked glasses.

"To the best Christmas ever," said Ida.

"Every Christmas is best to me," said Madeline.

"This year he's coming home. You wait and see."

"Lord. You're not starting with that again?"

"You'll see."

"Gonna get yourself all worked up," she said as she glanced at the silver-framed photograph of Ida's son that occupied the mantle. He was so handsome in his uniform. "You know Mr. Donald is not coming home."

Ida brushed her hand through the air, dismissing Madeline's warning. She pulled the angel from the box and walked over to the short ladder Madeline had out and ready for trimming the tree.

"Oh, no, you're not. You know heights make you dizzy. Give me that."

Madeline took the angel and climbed the ladder, hearing it squeak under her weight. How many times, she thought, as she reached up to put the angel into place? How many times had she lifted the little boy holding this same angel, his arms extended, to the top of the tree when he insisted on helping? She could still feel his weight. Tears filled her eyes, and she stopped for a moment unable to make out the top of the tree.

"Make sure it faces out toward the hallway. I want to see it when I come in," directed Ida.

Madeline blinked the tears away and twisted the ends. "Gonna be one of those days," she mumbled to herself, as Mr. Cole reached *Sing choirs of Angels* in the background.

CHAPTER TWO

Junior Thomas hesitated before opening the door to the apartment. The key was in the lock, but he paused to listen before going in. He hoped Queen was out. He resented her sudden reappearance. He knew he shouldn't, but he did.

Hearing no sounds, he turned the key and opened the door. He detected a trace of her cheap perfume mixed with the familiar musky odor of the old apartment, but he entered anyway, closing the door behind him. He picked up the small stack of mail sitting on the hall table, sorting through it and tossing the ads and pleas for funds into the trash. All that was left was the phone bill.

"Junior! That you?" came his grandmother's frail voice from the back bedroom.

"Yes, Gramma."

"You all right?"

Junior smiled. She was forever asking if he was all right, as if she expected some harm to visit him. Eula Thomas was a worrier.

"I'm fine. I'll be back there in a minute."

He slipped his forefinger beneath the end of the flap

and zipped open the envelope. A tiny slit of a paper cut gritted his teeth, and he shook his hand to counter the sting. As he sucked on his finger for further relief, the large red letters scrawled across the bottom of the phone bill shouted PAST DUE at him. A frown crumpled his handsome dark brown face. Pulling the damp finger from his mouth, he mumbled, "Past due?" He looked up, shaking his head knowingly, and marched down the hall to his grandmother's bedroom. As he passed Queen's door, he heard her inside snoring softly.

Eula's broad smile and sparkling chestnut eyes greeted Junior, dissolving his frown. She was like a puppy, he thought, always worried when he was away and always glad to see him return.

"How was class?"

"Fine, Gramma. Just fine," he hesitated a moment. "Gramma, you didn't pay the phone bill. Did you forget?"

"No. Mae paid it," she said, using Queen's given name.

Unable to control his reaction, Junior slammed his right fist into the palm of his left hand, crushing the phone bill it held. A single drop of blood from the cut smeared the bill. "I told you not to give her any money."

"What's the matter?"

"This," he waived the bill in the air. "This is what's the matter. It's past due."

"Must be some mistake."

"Mistake, all right. The mistake was giving Queen money."

"I wish you wouldn't call her that name. She's your mother."

"Yeah. Well, every john on the street calls her Queen, and you know it."

"Don't," she extended her arm, the palm of her hand pumping the air in a warning. "I don't want to hear that kinda talk about my baby."

Junior watched his grandmother's eyes fill with tears and wished he hadn't reacted so violently. He walked over to her bed and sat down on the edge, taking her frail brown hand in his and hearing the old box spring give a moan. He could smell the Noxzema she rubbed into her face each morning, hoping to stave off the ever-growing wrinkles. Her hand was smooth and soft.

"Do you still have your Social Security check?"

Eula looked away for a moment and wiped the tears with her free right hand. She just knew he would ask her about her Social Security check. "Mae cashed it for me. She paid the rent, the phone bill and the electricity," she turned back, tilting her head to make sure he could see her eyes. "I tell you it's some kind of bookkeeping error. The phone company is bad about those things." She squeezed her grandson's hand, signaling the strength of her belief.

"What about the rest of the money?"

"Just two hundred left, after the bills. You know that."

"She give it back?" he said, already knowing the answer.

"She borrowed it. Gonna pay me back on Friday."

Junior whistled a long sigh, squinching his eyes closed and shaking his head. "Listen, Gramma, you cannot give Queen any more money. She's got a habit. She shoots up every cent she gets her hands on."

"She's off that stuff, Junior. She's trying to find a job. She'll pay me back," she said, dipping her chin, an outward sign to herself that he'd be wrong. "You'll see."

He knew it was useless to argue with her. She refused to believe that her daughter was nothing but a prostitute and junkie.

"Okay. We'll see. But you can't give her any more money. You hear?"

With another moan from the springs, Junior rose from the bed and bent down to kiss her on the forehead, feeling the tingle of Noxzema on his lips and brushing his hand across them. He knew what the outcome would be, and he hated seeing her get hurt again.

"I gotta get to work now. You want me to turn on the television?"

"That'd be nice. Hard to get out of bed today."

Junior turned on the old black-and-white set, adjusting the knobs to keep the picture from rolling. He knew what channel to select. He knew she loved her afternoon soap operas.

"I'm gonna check this out with Queen now. So don't go getting all worked up if she overreacts."

"Leave her sleep, Junior. She needs her rest."

"And we need to know that the phone bill was paid. That was all the money we had."

Junior tapped on the door of his mother's room and waited for a moment. It was his room really, but she had reclaimed it on her return from the long absence, sending him back to the sofa bed he found painfully uncomfortable. She didn't answer, so he opened it and went in. He could see her wrapped tightly in the bedding and knew she'd been sleeping fitfully. He tapped her shoulder lightly and, getting no response, he shook her a little harder. Queen snorted and rolled over to open one bloodshot eye. Junior could smell the stale cigarettes and gin as she licked her lips and rubbed back her matted black hair. Without saying anything, she closed the open eye and rolled back over.

Junior shook her violently. "Queen! Queen! Wake up, dammit."

She rolled over again and managed to prop herself up on one elbow, rubbing her hand across her mouth, the blanket falling to expose one firm, nut-brown breast. "You? What you want? Can't you see I'm not feelin' good?"

"You didn't pay the phone bill, did you?"

"Go away," she said, flopping back onto the pillow,

the exposed breast spreading out and falling to the side.

"Tell me the truth. I know you didn't pay it."

"You don't know nothin'," she snarled.

"Anything. You don't know anything."

"Goddamn smartass. Get the hell outta here. Can't stand your sorry black ass," she said, slurring her words, angry at being both challenged and corrected by her son.

"Where is the rest of her money?"

Queen rolled over and pulled the covers over her head. He could hear his grandmother calling him from her bedroom. His fists were clinched tightly and he could feel the blood pulsing through his head. With a sigh of exasperation, he turned and left the room.

CHAPTER THREE

Madeline hummed a nameless tune as she carefully washed the breakfast dishes. It always made Ida smile, hearing her hum precisely the same notes even though there was no such song. Somehow Madeline had committed the self-composed melody to memory. She'd taught it to Ida's son as a little boy on the grand piano in the living room, and they would play it over and over in duet. Wiping each plate carefully as Madeline handed them to her, Ida wondered what her housekeeper's life would have been like had she not come to work for her nearly fifty years ago. She was bright. She could play hundreds of tunes on the piano from memory, not just popular ditties but classics as well. She could have been almost anything had her options not been limited by her position in life. Still, Ida was glad she was here.

"Wish I'd studied the piano like my momma wanted me to," said Ida, looking over at Madeline.

"Never told me you wanted to play the piano. What brought that to mind?"

"Oh, I suppose your humming. It'd be nice to be able to work out the notes, you know? You taught Donald to play it. Could have taught me, too. It's such a nice tune.

Somebody might pay money for a tune like that."

Madeline laughed, secretly enjoying the compliment, her ample breasts bouncing with each chuckle. "Frivolous," she said, bobbing her head to mimic her mother's recalled assessment of the tune. "My mamma said anything outside of a hymn was frivolous. Didn't want me playing anywhere but church."

"Didn't your mother want you to have a career in music? She must have seen your talent."

"Career?" Madeline said, turning to Ida with a *have-you-lost-your-mind* look. "A black girl in the thirties with a sixth grade education? Honky-tonk piano in some dive, maybe. But a career?" Madeline laughed weakly, sadly. Ida averted her eyes, picking up another plate and rubbing it furiously. Madeline knew she felt awkward. "Only thing my mamma wanted back then was me out of the house. 'Sides, no one's gonna buy my little ditty. Rock, acid rock is what sells these days."

"Well, I still think it's awfully pretty."

"If you're serious, I'll teach you to play it."

The thought of taking a lesson from meticulous Madeline gave Ida pause. "Pie smells good," she said, anxious to change the topic. She inhaled the sweet-tart smell of Madeline's apple pie baking in the oven and was about to offer another compliment when the doorbell rang. She wiped her hands. "I'll get it," she said, setting the dishtowel down on the counter. "Probably those two girls about the guest house."

Pushing open the swinging door to the hall, she could see the girls' rippled outlines in the bottle-glass window of the door. She peered into the living room as she passed to admire the Christmas tree and took another deep breath, appreciating the pine scent even more on the tree's second day in the house.

"He'll be here," she whispered to herself. "This year, he'll be here."

She struggled to pull the door open and a whoosh of

trapped air escaped the house. She could see one girl's nostrils flare as she appreciated the aroma of Madeline's pie.

"Something smells good!" the young woman said with a big smile. "Apple pie, I bet?"

"You'd bet right, too," said Ida.

"I'm Louise," said the good guesser. "And this is Judy. We called you about the guest house."

"Ida. Ida Hanson. Yes. Well, let's go round the back, and I'll show it to you," she said, pointing down the steps.

They descended the steps in unison, turning right to make their way up the cracked surface of the drive leading to the back of the house. Louise was the outgoing one, Ida thought as they walked together, ducking the limbs of an overgrown hibiscus that skirted the driveway. Her long blonde hair, too-short skirt, and easy speech spoke of her bubbly nature. Ida guessed she was a Sagittarian. Judy, on the other hand, wore slacks with her hair cut in a short pixie-like style, and remained silent. Ida wasn't sure of her sign. Still, silence was not a bad thing in Ida's book.

When they reached the back yard, Ida pointed to the old garage. "It's over there. Attached to the garage." For a moment, she was embarrassed by the peeling paint on the trim of the garage and guest house. "Gonna have some painting done soon, of course."

She noticed Judy hesitate for a few seconds before following them to the guest house door. "My houseman died last year. Been vacant since then," Ida said as she inserted the key into the lock. "He drove for me, too."

The two girls watched as Ida fiddled with the key, lifting up and down on the doorknob. The bolt made a hollow knock as it finally gave way. Ida turned the knob, but the door would not open. She leaned into it, but it still resisted the intrusion.

"Maybe you can help me," she said, smiling

nervously at the silent Judy who stood next to her. "Gets a little warped from time to time."

Judy added her weight to the door and it shuttered open. "There," said Ida, reaching in to switch on the lights. "Lack of use is all it is."

She stepped in and the two girls followed somewhat reluctantly. The sudden rush of air from the open door sent particles of dust floating across the broad spread of light coming from the old silk-shaded floor lamp. Judy eyed the faded rose color of the lampshade, her lip curling involuntarily. Ida opened the drapes, shedding more light on the dust that covered every surface of the somewhat dated furniture in the crowded little room. The girls eyed each other, knowing it wasn't what they wanted. It was dark and smelled musky like the rundown hotel they had been staying in for the past two weeks.

"I'll have it dusted before you move in. Haven't had the nerve to open it up for awhile. I miss old Arthur, you see? But it will be clean as a whistle when you move in."

It was Judy who mustered the strength to speak first. "I'm afraid it's not what we expected for $1,700.00. It's... it's nice and all. Don't get me wrong. It's just not what we expected."

A Leo, Ida thought.

"But you haven't seen the bedrooms. Got two nice-sized bedrooms and a kitchenette."

"We don't want to waste your time. Really, we just can't see paying that much money for... for, well, this. I'm sorry," said Judy, offering a weak smile.

I liked her better when she was silent, thought Ida.

"Well, perhaps we could discuss the price? I could maybe make a little adjustment, provided, that is, you wouldn't mind doing a few things around here."

"Things?" said Judy, looking doubtful.

"You know. A little painting. Maybe some yard work."

Both girls looked horror stricken. "We've taken too

much of your time already. Thank you," said Judy, turning and heading for the door.

"Yes, thank you. Mrs. Hanson," said Louise.

"Well, if you change your mind..." Ida began, but it was too late. Both girls had walked out.

Ida stopped to look around the room before pulling the door closed. She imagined Arthur sitting in his favorite chair watching television. She blinked him away and closed the door, pulling hard to make sure it was secure.

Madeline was in the kitchen scraping carrots when Ida came back in. She glanced up and knew the girls had declined by the look on Ida's face. Didn't get her way, she thought, but said nothing.

"We need to do some dusting out there," Ida said. "You have remembered to start the car every week?"

"Yes. Twice a week. I remembered. That's the second time this week you've asked me."

"Wouldn't want the battery going dead."

"I don't suppose you'd reconsider hiring another man?"

"Tried to. You know that. I tried to," grumped Ida.

"Need to offer more money. People earn decent money these days."

"Arthur was perfectly happy with what I paid him."

"Yes. And Arthur was a saint. Aren't many saints looking to drive old ladies to the grocery store these days."

"Humph!" said Ida as she walked past Madeline and out the swinging door.

CHAPTER FOUR

In spite of the cool day, perspiration trickled down Junior's forehead as he sat on the low wall behind Ben's Burgers, taking his lunch break. He wore the required white company shirt with its embarrassing, shocking orange sleeves and collar that Ben had designed himself. The odor of greasy hamburger, mixed with the rancid fat from the French fryer that bubbled away all day, rose up from the clothing it had permeated to choke him. He wished this was one of his short days, but Friday was 9 to 5.

He took a long sip of his soda and set it down beside him, wondering if he should try to get off early. For the past two afternoons, Queen had slipped out before he could make it home. And even though his grandmother had promised to confront her, Junior knew she just wouldn't or couldn't do it. He needed to know that at least the rent had been paid. If the phone was shut off, they could live with that. He was pretty sure the electric company didn't cut off the service until at least 60 days had gone by without receiving payment, or so he'd heard. But their rent was another story, and he had shied away from calling the landlord, not wanting to hear it hadn't been paid. The trouble with taking off early was it meant a leaner paycheck. And, if nothing had been paid, they'd need every dime he could scrape together.

"Dammit," he said to himself, picking up the soda for another sip. Why had she come back? Why would she do this to her own mother?

Behind him, the rusted old spring on Ben's screen door made a metallic screech followed by a resounding slam as the door smacked shut. Junior looked over to see his friend Edgar ambling his way. He held a milk shake in one hand and a package of cigarettes in the other. He was lanky and walked like the storks Junior had seen on *Wild Kingdom*, his head bobbed with each step, his torso did a slight roll and his arms swayed back and forth alternately with each step. He was a bit goofy, but he'd attached himself to Junior long ago when Junior skipped a grade, moving from fifth directly into seventh. He'd been too bright for his classmates, but in jumping ahead he found himself lost among the older students. It had been Edgar, awkward even then, who had befriended Junior, and he was just about the only friend Junior trusted.

Edgar sat down on the wall next to him with his long legs jackknifed and spread apart at the knee as his bony elbows did a chicken-flapping motion, one brushing Junior's sleeve. Junior couldn't see his hands, somewhere at crotch level, but he assumed Edgar was struggling to open the package of cigarettes. His face was all concentration. When one hand finally did appear, Edgar was shaking a cigarette out of the mauled opening. He offered it to Junior.

"Bad for your health," said Junior.

"So's that shit," Edgar said, pointing at the half-eaten hamburger Junior held in his hand.

Junior looked at the remains of the burger. "Yeah. You're probably right." He pitched it across the driveway into an open dumpster and wiped the residual grease from his hands on a paper napkin, wadding it into a ball and tossing it after the burger. "When I'm a doctor, I'll never eat hamburgers and French fries again."

"Amen, brother. I figure it'll take at least six months to get the smell out of my nose hairs."

They sat silently for a few minutes, watching the traffic flash by on Martin Luther King Boulevard. Edgar slurped up the last few noisy drops of his milkshake and, feeling antsy, got up to dance awkwardly to an imagined tune. Junior rolled his eyes and smiled to himself. There was just something funny about every movement Edgar made, but he had to give him credit for never feeling self-conscious. After awhile, Edgar switched to shadow boxing, punching Junior in the arm several times with his long reach.

"Stop it, Edgar."

But Edgar didn't listen. He threw several punches at an imagined opponent and then jabbed Junior again.

"I said leave me alone! Dammit! Got too much on my mind to be playing silly-assed games."

Edgar slowed his fancy footwork and finally stopped. "What's bugging you, man? Got trouble with the ladies?"

Junior ignored his questions, looking down, shaking his head. Edgar, like most of the guys he knew, thought of nothing but "the ladies", as they called them.

"Is it 'cause your mamma came home?" When Junior didn't answer, he added, "Saw her on Slauson gettin' in some white dude's Cadillac yesterday."

"So?" Junior said, narrowing his eyes and staring at Edgar.

"So, nothin'. Don't have to talk about it if you don't feel like it."

Junior shrugged. Edgar eyed him carefully, waiting for a response of some kind. But Junior said nothing. Edgar wished he hadn't told him about Queen picking up a trick. He didn't know why he'd mentioned it.

Trying to recover the ground he'd lost, Edgar asked, "You going to the mall after work?"

"Shopping? For what?"

"Christmas, Junior. You am a Christian?"

"Are. You are a Christian," Junior corrected him, even though he knew Edgar understood the difference and had merely lapsed into his jive talk. Junior hated jive talk.

Edgar absent-mindedly shot the finger at him. "The mall will be hopping tonight. Chicks will be on the lookout, too. I'm goin'. Wanna come?"

"Nah. I don't need anything from the mall."

"Junior, my man. Need has nothing to do with it. Chicks. You hear? C-H-I-C-K-S," Edgar spelled it out.

"No thanks."

Edgar liked Junior and, despite his lack of response, he would not give up on the conversation. "If it's money, I've got it. I'll spring for dinner."

"It's not money. Chicks and money are the only things you think about," he said, glancing up at Edgar, who smiled back at him. A simple soul, he thought. Why did he let Edgar bug him? He realized then that he wasn't being very nice to him, and decided to join in the conversation. "I'm saving to buy Gramma a color television for Christmas. That old black-and-white is on its last legs. Otherwise, I'd go with you," he said, trying not to disappoint Edgar without letting him in on why the little money he did have would have to be stretched thanks to Queen.

"Color TV? Whoa. Mister spender. Gonna cost you some big ones."

"Yeah. I've been putting away $10.00 a week. Got $380.00 saved up. It won't be a very big one. But at least it will work and have a remote control."

"Want me to go with you?" asked Edgar, eager to be included in anything Junior did.

Ben leaned out the back door and signaled Junior

his lunch break was up. Junior waived a hand at him and smiled.

"No, thanks. Can't go until Monday when I get paid." Junior said, getting up and starting for the door.

"What are you gettin' your mamma for Christmas?"

"Queen? Humph. A bus ticket if she'd take it."

CHAPTER FIVE

At one o'clock, Ida walked down the stairs quietly, not wanting to let Madeline hear her until it was too late for her to defeat Ida's planned shopping trip. After their discussion about a replacement for Arthur, she certainly didn't want Madeline tagging along. She crossed the hall and opened the closet door. The hinges squeaked slightly; it was barely perceptible to the human ear. But before she could get her mink coat out, she heard the swinging door flying open. Ida winced.

"You goin' out? Didn't tell me you were goin' out."

Ida closed the closet door and walked over to the hall table. "Just a little shopping to do. Be back by four, five at the latest," she said as she slipped into her knee-length fur coat, inhaling the lightly medicinal odor of the moth balls rising from it.

Madeline shook her head. "I'll call you a cab."

"Don't need a cab. I'm taking the bus."

"The bus!" Madeline said aghast. "It's not safe."

"Nonsense. Used to ride the bus downtown all the time."

"Forty years ago."

"I like riding the bus."

"You haven't been on a bus since before you hired Arthur. And you know it."

"It's perfectly safe. You worry too much."

Madeline made a beeline to the closet and pulled out a cloth coat. She walked back with it, draped it over her arm and lifted Ida's fur from behind by the collar. "Not in that coat, you're not." She felt Ida tighten her grip on the old coat. "Get hit over the head. Don't you read the papers? People spit on fur coat wearers these days. 'Sides, that coat'd be too warm if the sun comes out."

Ida shrugged, releasing her grip and allowing the coat to be taken from her. She calculated that if she relented on this battle, she'd have a better chance of getting out the door without Madeline and without taking a cab.

"If you wait ten minutes, my pie will be done and I can go along. Take a cab that long to get here anyway."

Ida adjusted her hat in the mirror over the table, picked up her purse and gloves and headed for the front door. "Haven't got time to wait around for you," she said, grasping the doorknob. She looked over her shoulder at Madeline who was frowning. She had hoped to swoop out dramatically, but when she twisted the doorknob, it came off in her hand as it often did. "Rats," she said in low voice.

Madeline walked over to the table and opened the drawer. She withdrew an overly large screwdriver and joined Ida at the door. "Give it here," she said, reaching for the knob. Ida handed it to her and she carefully pushed it back into place. As she bent down to tighten the screw, Ida stuck her tongue out at her. "I saw that," said Madeline, not looking up. They both chuckled.

"We need a man around this house," Madeline said, turning the screwdriver with great concentration.

"When Donald gets home, he'll fix everything."

Madeline shook her head as she straightened up and backed away from the door. "That's what you're up too, isn't it? Gonna buy him another Christmas present."

Ida pulled the door open and walked out onto the porch. "None of your business what I'm gonna buy. Just need some things." She walked down the steps.

"Not takin' a whole lotta cash, are you?" shouted Madeline. Remember. We're not exchanging gifts this year. We agreed."

"Agreed to no such thing. Mind your pie."

~*~

It was four blocks to Wilshire Boulevard, and Ida strolled along at a good clip. With the fresh smell of a newly mown lawn she passed, her nostrils flared as she breathed in deeply. She thought that if she closed her eyes, it could be autumn in Evanston, Illinois instead of an overcast December in Los Angeles. Even the large houses on Hudson Street reminded her of the neighborhood she grew up in. Each of the homes here in Hancock Park had been custom built, mostly in the thirties and forties for the stars, studio executives and oil-money families with an occasional doctor and lawyer thrown in. She liked walking through the neighborhood, pretending she was somewhere else, someone else.

"Let's see," she said softly to herself. "Today, I'll be a movie star out for a shopping spree. Make that a thirty year old Lana Turner." With that, she stopped to open her purse and dig out her sunglasses, picturing herself with blonde hair drawn up into a French roll and her cloth coat in leopard skin. She dug around for a moment and finally located them, but to her surprise one lens was cracked and ready to pop from the frame. So she changed her mind. Today, she'd have to be Ida Hanson; a thirty year old Ida Hanson, though.

She snapped her purse shut and was about to proceed when the sun peeked through the clouds momentarily, catching a shiny object laying on the street next to the curb. "A lucky penny," she thought, and she walked over and stepped off the curb. She looked both ways to ensure no one was looking and bent down. The penny was half embedded in the blacktop surface, but she tenaciously dug one fingernail under it and pried it up. She straightened up, tucked the penny in her purse, and returned to the sidewalk.

"Gonna be a lucky day," she said to herself.

At the corner of Hudson and Wilshire, she crossed the street, quickening her pace to reach the other side before the light changed, and walked to the bus bench. She stopped to catch her breath before sitting down. An advertisement for a funeral parlor was plastered across the back of the bench. She wondered why it was that a funeral parlor should have to advertise and, of all places, on a bus stop, but let the thought go. The seat of the bench was spattered with what looked to be dried vomit, so she stood next to the bus stop to wait, hoping she wasn't downwind. A little shiver of excitement raced through her small frame as she stood on the busy corner waiting for the bus, and she smiled.

CHAPTER SIX

The piercing glare of the reflected light in the windows of the little shops blinded Queen as she made her way along Slauson. The light of day, even with an overcast sky, was too much for her eyes, the pupils still dilated from whatever it was she'd had the night before. She pulled the red-framed sunglasses from her horse feeder-shaped handbag and guided them into place without slowing her progress. She had a splitting headache. She needed to score soon, or the shakes would seize control of her limbs and diminish her resolve. She kept one eye on the passing cars, hoping Dino or Skeet would drive by. They were the only two dealers in the area not under Cato's control.

Queen knew that when Cato found out, there would be hell to pay. And for once she blamed herself. She only wished her mother hadn't asked her to get the damn check cashed. She'd only asked for a hundred, or was it two, she couldn't remember. The next thing she knew it was all gone, after promising herself she wouldn't do it to her again. But it was gone, and she now knew she had no choice.

Her head ached and even the events of an hour ago

seemed foggy now as she moved closer to the shops, seeking less light. She barely remembered Cato handing her the bag and telling her where to meet The Reverend "C", a regular customer, in the park. But she did remember her hair being yanked back and his mean eyes as he warned her. For the first time in the six months she'd been back, he was trusting her to carry. And she'd done exactly as she was told, signaling the cautious minister, watching him place the envelope behind the water fountain and switching the bag for the envelope. And then, as she crossed the park, a patrol car had appeared from nowhere. It was just cruising and hadn't seen the switch, but she didn't know that. She'd panicked, struggling to run on rubber legs, stumbling and trying to catch herself with one hand that missed its targeted bench rail. She'd rolled over several times in the grass, coming to rest beneath the broad spread of a hibiscus bush in full red flower, the money from the envelope scattered about her. By the time she'd caught her breath, the patrol car was gone.

She stayed there beneath the bush for a while, lying on her back and waiting for the shakes to pass, seeing Cato's hands in her hair and her mother's sad eyes, and she made a snap decision. She had to get out. Things had to change.

She attempted, once again, to shake the morning's horror from her head and stepped forward with new resolve. Approaching the corner, she spotted a patrol car turning left onto Slauson two blocks ahead. She quickly ducked into the entrance alcove of a key shop and opened the door. A little bell rang, signaling her entrance, and an old black man came to the front counter. She could hear him wheezing from behind her.

"Can I help you?"

Queen's head bounced furtively back and forth between the street view and the old man. "No. No, Pops. Just stepped in from the sun for a minute. I'm a little dizzy."

The old man frowned. Sun? He thought. And he stared at her for a moment until he placed her face and recognized the tight, mid-thigh black skirt and low-cut blouse. He'd seen her countless times at work on this street, the cars stopping, Queen bending down to negotiate.

"Cops?"

Queen eyed him suspiciously, then smiled. "Yeah. Cops, Pop." She watched him smile and wink. "Sorry."

"Nah. Nothing to be sorry for," he said. "You'd think they'd have something better to do."

"Need a little action?" Queen said, shifting her weight to one hip, throwing back her shoulders to show off her ample breasts. It was a reflex action, asking and posing, and she suddenly felt programmed. She wasn't really interested in scoring today. She had other plans.

"Nah. Mrs. Pop'd have my hide," he smiled and motioned with his head to the back room.

Queen smiled back and winked, relieved that he'd not taken the bait. From the corner of her eye, she saw the patrol car pass by. "Coast is clear. Thanks," she said, opening the door and walking out.

She looked both ways before continuing down the street. Her hand automatically slipped into her handbag, feeling for the envelope. It was there. The money made her nervous. Cato's money. She knew she had only a couple of hours to escape. Three, maybe. She was sure Cato would soon be looking for her, but she needed something, anything, a little smack, even some weed. Just something to cut the edge before she headed out.

A shutter passed through her and her vision blurred slightly. She stopped and closed her eyes for a moment, leaning against a storefront window. She could hear her son's voice, "Where is it? Where's the money?" She mumbled, "Smartass," hating his smugness, his hatred of her. "He'll see," she said, surprisingly loud. And then more softly, "He'll see." But she was beginning to doubt her resolve. Could she pull it off? She wasn't sure. She shook her head, forcing her eyes to open, and staggered along until her vision returned. She needed something. Needed it now.

CHAPTER SEVEN

The hydraulic hiss of the bus brakes being pumped signaled its jerky stop. The passengers lining up behind Ida to get off shoved her forward, making her exit awkward. She leaned back to stave off their aggression, and carefully made her way down the steps to the curb. Once there, the passengers pushed her aside in their rush to get wherever they were headed. Rude, thought Ida as she pulled her open coat closed and grasped her handbag tightly in front of her.

The bus pulled away, trailed by a sooty-black smoke that engulfed Ida. She choked up a cough and her eyes burned. She blinked several times and then closed her eyes and stopped breathing to fend off the diesel fumes.

She thought of London and the predominate diesel-scented air that accompanied her everywhere she went on that last trip they'd made in '51, the trip that had taken Jack from her. She could still see the striped pavement, the zebra crossing, as the English called it. She remembered his quick glance to the left before stepping from the curb despite the printed warning to LOOK RIGHT. But her visual memory always stopped there, stopped before the hurtling, bulky black shape of the cab, the screech of brakes, the dull and fatal thump. The vision was blocked but not the sounds. Intentional perhaps, but thankfully blocked.

"Are you all right?" came the soft voice accompanied by the light pressure of a hand on Ida's elbow.

Ida opened her eyes, finding a tall blonde woman of maybe thirty tilting her head downward with a concerned look on her face. The crowd and bus fumes had dispersed.

"Oh. Oh, yes. Yes, fine. Thank you."

"You looked a bit pale. Are you sure you're okay?

"Just the bus fumes. A bit overpowering. Thank you though."

The woman smiled but looked unconvinced. "Right," she said and walked on down the pavement, looking back after a few steps, still doubting Ida's response.

Ida mustered a broad grin to reassure her and stepped out at a quick pace toward the entrance to Macy's department store. She heard the repetitive tinkling of a tiny bell before she saw the very skinny impersonation of Santa Claus standing in front of the entrance. Next to him stood a familiar Salvation Army collection pot hanging from a tripod. She chuckled at seeing such a sad rendition of Santa. He had a bushy white beard that hung askew and an incongruously black mustache. Then she noticed he had no hat. What was Santa without the hat?

She opened her purse, fished out a $5 bill and approached. She abruptly stopped in front of him, noticing the "Seasons Greetings" sign affixed to the pot. Her fist tightened around the bill, crushing it.

"Season's Greetings? What happened to Merry Christmas?" she said with a snarl.

Santa only shrugged. So Ida released her tight grip on the $5 bill and crammed it into the little pot.

"A very Merry Christmas to you," he said with a broad smile.

Ida smiled back. "That's more like it," and she turned to walk away.

"Ms-s-s-s," he added smugly.

Ida winced but ignored his little joke and proceeded through the doors and into the store, stopping for a moment to get her bearings.

The place was alive with shoppers. She could hear sound of Christmas carols piped over the music system as it floated from all sides. Ida loved big stores, everything new, everything stacked neatly, especially good stores. They always smelled expensively of promised treasures. She wandered through the cosmetics section and a young woman sprayed her with some new fragrance. It was far too sweet for her tastes but passable, she thought.

At the base of the escalator she found the store directory. The men's section was on the top floor. She mounted the moving steps with some hesitation, having read about shoes getting caught in the crevices, and let the metal steps whisk her on high.

When she reached the top floor, the escalator seemed to spit her out. Her little feet did a rough shuffle to compensate for the momentum that had taken her by surprise. She caught her breath and looked around. The floor was very quiet compared to the rest of the store. She could see only one other shopper and no salespeople. She figured its location, so far above everything else, eliminated passers-through.

From behind her came a decidedly male voice, a baritone. "May I help you?"

Ida turned to see a tall blond young man of perhaps thirty. His eyes were a marvelously clear light blue color.

She found herself speechless in his presence. He was very handsome, lean and broad-shouldered and dressed in dark blue. She felt her heart flutter like a young girl.

"May I show you something?"

Ida's face flushed with embarrassment, but she

mustered a reply. "A sweater, please. A cardigan, I think?" and she smiled.

"Yes. This way, please," he said, pointing the direction and taking the lead.

Ida followed him. Her feet glided easily over the highly polished marble floors, but they were beginning to hurt. Should have worn older shoes, she thought, as she hurried to keep up with the young man. When they reached the sweater counter, he walked behind it and turned to face Ida. He leaned forward and smiled, showing perfectly spaced, bright white teeth. Ida wondered if he was working here while awaiting a call from one of the studios. If he wasn't an actor, he should be. She noticed his nametag said Myron. Not a good name for an actor, she thought.

"Did you have a color in mind?"

"Color? Oh, yes. Let's see. Green or, perhaps, dark blue."

Myron bent down and pulled out a green cardigan, opening it and laying it flat on the counter. "How about this one? 100% lamb's wool, but surprisingly soft," he said, running his hand over the sleeve. She noticed that his nails were perfectly manicured just as her husband's had always been. "We also have a cashmere if you'd prefer it? A bit pricey, though."

Ida felt the sweater's smooth surface and noticed the price tag, $65.00. "Let's see the cashmere. Just for the heck of it," she said, not wanting to seem impoverished, wishing Madeline hadn't taken her mink. "It's for my son, you see. For Christmas."

"Yes, of course," said Myron, turning around and taking a stack of cashmere sweaters from the case behind him. "Here we are. And the size?"

"Oh. He's about your size, I guess."

"I take a large." Myron began leafing through the sweaters, looking for the proper size. "Will you be joining you for Christmas then?" he said, making small talk.

"I really can't say. I hope so, but he's in Vietnam."

"Vietnam? On business?"

"Why, no. The war, of course."

"The war?" Myron said, wrinkling his brow.

"Yes, the war."

"The war with Vietnam?" Myron gave Ida a queer look, wondering if she was operating on all cylinders. He thought it best to humor Ida. "Oh... Oh, yes. That war." Myron gulped noticeably and held up a navy blue cardigan. He didn't really see, but knew better than to get embroiled in a lengthy conversation.

~*~

Maria Mendoza held the cool damp paper towel against her closed eyelids, tilting her head back and making a sniffling sound as she willed herself to stop crying. The bulge of her lower abdomen spread over the porcelain basin as she leaned against it for support. Twenty minutes of tormented tears had left her nasal passages clogged and her eyes swollen and red. She wanted to move beyond it now, wanted to stop the useless crying.

Lifting the towel from her face, she shook her head slowly, whispering, "Twelve years." Maria saw her usually pretty face in the mirror and was instantly sadder for its puffiness and blotchy, tear-streaked makeup. "How can they do this to me?" she said. She blew her nose in the paper towel and poked it through the water-spotted chrome flap of the trash bin. She sniffled.

For twelve happy years, she had quietly gone about her job, opening, sorting and distributing the mail at first on a part-time basis. Then, after a year of night school to perfect her English, she'd taken over the switchboard as well as the mail and helped with the ever-increasing load of typing for the firm. She was proud of her work and everyone here liked her. She knew it. She had two gold-framed certificates of appreciation hanging on the wall behind her desk to prove it.

"Don't know what we'd do without you, Maria," she mumbled to her reflection, repeating the words she had heard so often from the lawyers. "Yeah. Sure," she said. "Merry Christmas."

It was the computer she blamed as she stood there trying to collect herself. It had all started with the computer that allowed for standardized text to be easily inserted into any letter or document, legalese. She'd hadn't noticed the impact of it at first. It had taken a while before the requests for her help in typing by the secretaries began to diminish. By then, they had hired a young man to handle the incoming and outgoing mail. And even though she'd asked, there seemed to be nothing to fill the slow times on the switchboard.

Maria blamed the new office manager, the evil Ruth, short and compact with prematurely gray hair. At first she seemed fine, seemed to fit into the picture, taking her time to get acquainted with everyone. But three months into her tenure, she'd started monitoring "work flow," as she called it. She began having everyone record things, numbers of letters, numbers of phone calls and paper and envelopes and anything measurable. She moved desks, moved files, moved everything around until Maria found her familiar environment suddenly strange and unsettling.

"Automated! Ha!" she grumbled to the mirror. It was just another computer to answer the phone. And now she had two weeks' severance thanks to Ruth, thanks to the computer.

The bathroom door eased open quietly, so quietly that Maria didn't hear it or see Ruth step in until her image appeared behind hers in the mirror. Maria jumped.

"It's time you gathered your things and went home

now, Maria," Ruth said softly. Her face reflected the painfulness of the task she'd preformed, but Maria saw it as phony. Maria made no reply. "I'm sorry we had to do this. I know you must be in shock."

Maria continued to stare at her, refusing to let her off the hook by saying something equally phony like *I'm sure*, or *It's okay. I understand.* She wasn't about to.

~*~

Eula closed her tattered old Bible and set it down on the bed beside her. She lifted her right leg which had fallen asleep and wiggled her toes. She was having a bad day. She grimaced as her arthritis-swollen knees and ankles fought the movement she imposed on them. She had dressed for the day, hoping to pay a visit to Alvin Burke who lived two doors down the hall, but she just didn't have the energy. She knew Alvin would be worried about her because he hadn't seen her for several days. But today, she just didn't have the strength.

From the front of the apartment, the top lock made its usual clunk as it was disengaged. Cocking her head, she heard a key fishing for home, then turning in the lock and the front door opening. She took a deep breath. She dreaded having to ask her daughter about the money she had loaned her two days ago, but she'd promised Junior she would. She heard the door close quietly and waited. Drawers were opened and closed in rapid succession, another door opened, and then another. Her heart beat faster, wondering if maybe it wasn't Mae, if perhaps it was a burglar.

She gulped hard and mustered her courage. "Mae, baby? That you, Mae?"

"Yes, Mamma," came her daughter's sigh-inducing reply.

"Come talk with me."

"Busy, Mamma. Late for an appointment already."

Ida sensed an edge in her daughter's voice. "Please,

baby. Come see me."

"Dammit! I said I was busy!" Queen yelled.

Eula's eyes widened, darting back and forth. She didn't want to have a scene. She knew the signs. She knew Mae was in one of her moods and it usually ended with a blowup.

Queen was busy stuffing her few belongings into the stiff new canvas duffle bag she'd picked up after sharing two joints with Dino. It had taken the edge off. She knew it would, but she was still shaky. She ran her trembling right hand under the bed, scooping out two pairs of soiled panties, and stuffed them into the bag. As she got up from her knees, she remembered the coffee can and went to the closet. A part of her didn't want to take it, but she knew Cato's money wouldn't be enough. She had no choice.

The odd noises continued to baffle Eula. Was she straightening up her bedroom? She wanted to go see, but she knew it was best to stay out of Mae's way right now.

After a few minutes, she heard Mae walking heavily down the hall toward the front door. Was she leaving without coming to see her? Perhaps it was best. Then she heard Mae turn around and walk back down the hall toward Eula's door, fast-paced, heavy-footed steps. Eula winced, gritting her teeth, as Mae shoved open the door with a bang as it hit the far wall. Eula flinched.

"What is it, Mamma?" Queen snarled. "What do you want from me now?" It was her way of keeping her mother at a distance. She didn't want any more questions about the rent.

"Just a little lonely is all. Just wanted company."

Mae's face softened slightly and she took a deep breath. "Sorry, Mamma. Got an important appointment, or I'd sit for awhile. You understand?"

"Yes, surely I do."

"Your ankles are swollen."

"Yeah, baby. Took my pills, but they're not working."

"Keep your feet up then. I gotta go now."

"Mae?"

Mae rolled her eyes. "Yes, Mamma?"

"You will be here for Christmas dinner, won't you? You're not running off again."

"I guess, Mamma."

"Been three years since we all had Christmas together."

Queen's hand rose to rest on her hip and her eyes narrowed, "Don't forget a damn thing, do you, Mamma?"

"Now, baby, don't take offense. I was just..." but Queen was gone before she could finish.

Eula heard the front door slam.

CHAPTER EIGHT

Ida set the two heavy shopping bags down on the sidewalk to wait for the bus. She was pleased with herself, having found a silver-plated vanity set that would be perfect in Madeline's room. The brushes were made of fine boars' hair and the mirror was just the right size. She'd have to hide it until Christmas which wouldn't be easy, but it was perfect. And she thought Donald's new sweater would bring out the blue in his eyes. All in all a good day. But her arms were already tired and her feet were killing her. She wanted a nice cup of tea.

Looking at her watch, she realized it had taken longer than she'd thought it would. It was already 4:30. With luck, she'd be home by five or a little after. She knew Madeline would be hovering by the front door.

When the bus pulled to the curb, she hefted the bags and mounted the steps, struggling to lift her tired legs high enough to scale them. She set the bags down and handed the driver the $1.35 fare and asked, "You do stop at Hudson Street, don't you?"

"Have to transfer at Normandie. Quarter more," said the dyspeptic looking driver in a strong Middle Eastern accent that Ida could barely understand. He didn't bother to tell her that the bus coming behind him in five minutes when straight down Wilshire all the way into Santa Monica.

"Transfer? But I came straight here from Hudson?"

"I said, you have to transfer at Normandie," he snapped without explaining why.

Ida fished a quarter out of her purse and handed it to the driver. He tore a transfer ticket from a pad and handed it to her without looking. Ida snatched it up and with a frown hefted the shopping bags.

The driver accelerated quickly, and Ida did a little cha-cha-cha forward, stumbling and grabbing hold of the back of a seat to keep from falling. None of the other riders made a move to help her. They seemed to be watching, waiting for her to fall. Gathering her composure, she made her way down the aisle and sat down on the first empty bench, crowding her bags in close to her legs.

Ida took a deep breath, noticing the smell of dried urine and body odor that permeated the bus. She gagged slightly and swallowed back her nausea. The bus was filthy, with graffiti scrawled across the backs of the seats and etched into the glass. She tried to distract her thoughts from the odors by watching the traffic and buildings that passed by. After the wonderful smells in the store, she wasn't going to let the bus and its odors sour her otherwise good day.

Perhaps it was the rolling motion of the passing scenery or maybe the airlessness of the bus, but Ida found herself suddenly sleepy. Her head began to bob slightly as she fought nodding off. It was no use, though. Before long, her head dropped to rest on her chest, supported by the collar of her soft woolen coat. A little gibbering sound came from her moist lips as the unwanted sleep grew deeper.

When the bus driver pulled to an abrupt stop at the

corner of Normandie and Wilshire fifteen minutes later, he expected to let the old lady off. He looked into his rear view mirror, but couldn't see Ida sound asleep, sitting behind a broad-shouldered businessman. He shrugged, assuming she'd got off earlier, and pulled into traffic, turning left on Normandie.

Ida was still fast asleep.

~*~

The double doors of Ben's Burgers flew wide as Junior fled the rancid smells. He carried a small gym bag, which he shifted to his left hand as he made his way across the street. A block away, he ducked into an alley and set the bag down on the blacktop. He hated the company shirt that he was forced to wear, but never changed it before leaving work. He was convinced that opening the gym bag there would contaminate his street clothes. He quickly unbuttoned and removed the ridiculous shirt, took off his hat, and pulled his T-shirt over his head, bearing his hairless, muscular chest to the cool air. A carload of passing Mexican girls hooted and waved as if he were a stripper. He shot them the finger, regretting it immediately, thinking Edgar was wearing off on him.

Junior knelt, opened the gym bag and removed a fresh T-shirt which he pulled over his head. He took out a sweatshirt and put it on. Rolling up the company shirt and his rank-smelling T-shirt, he tucked them into the bag along with the hat and closed it.

Junior felt better now. He could still smell the French fries and hamburger grease, but it wasn't nearly as pungent. He glanced at his watch, exactly 5:05, and walked to the corner, crossed the· street, and took a seat on the bus bench at the corner of 54th and Normandie to wait for his bus. He hoped Queen would be home when he arrived. While he dreaded the confrontation with her, the money was too important to ignore.

~*~

Maria walked out of the high rise laden with the personal contents of her desk and file cabinets in a crumpled shopping bag. She had left the office through a back door, avoiding having to say good-bye to the lucky ones still gainfully employed by Hutchins & Hutchins. She'd walked away from twelve years of what she had hoped would be a lifetime career, knowing she had two weeks' severance, less than a month's salary in savings, fifty-one dollars and some odd change in her cookie jar and two young boys to support without a husband.

The day's overcast skies had continued into the early evening, which made it easier on her still swollen eyes. She'd done her best to restore her makeup, but her blood-shot eyes told the story. She stopped to remove a pair of sunglasses to hide her eyes from the world and walked on.

What would she tell her parents, she thought? She would no longer be able to send them the $100 money order each month, the money they depended on to buy the little extras to make their meager lives somewhat easier. A hundred U.S. dollars went a long way in their small border town near Nogales. She shook her head and picked up her pace. They were the least of her problems now.

When she reached the bus stop, she sat down on the bench and withdrew the large brown envelope Ruth had given her from her purse. She pulled out the papers and began to read the brochure: State of California, Employment Development Department. "*Your rights as a severed employee...* Severed," she whispered.

CHAPTER NINE

Junior made his way down the aisle as the bus pulled into traffic, grasping alternate seat backs to control his progress. The bus was crowded as usual, but there were a few seats left. He eased into a bench next to an old woman whose two shopping bags meant his feet remained in the aisle. The old woman was fast asleep, and he puzzled over her destination. He didn't often see well-dressed white women headed into South Central Los Angeles. He could smell the strangely sweet perfume she wore that somehow didn't suit her. Directly across from him a Mexican woman sneezed violently in his direction. He turned his face from her and wedged his feet, one atop the other, in under the bench ahead.

The bus bobbed from side to side under the weight of its load, and he watched the old woman's head sway in the opposite direction of its motion. Seventies, he guessed. He wished someone had told her to turn the stone of the diamond ring she wore around to hide it.

Junior was anxious to get home, and it seemed that the bus was making little progress. It inched along in heavy rush hour traffic, fighting after each stop to regain a position in the steady stream of cars headed south along Normandie. He hoped that when he got home he would be wrong about the money, hoped that somehow the phone company had made a mistake and that Queen had paid the rent and other bills. They could make it on what he had if she didn't repay the two hundred today, but he didn't want to face the thought of his grandmother's entire social security check being wasted on a few highs. Where would they get the rent?

He was staring straight ahead when a Korean woman across the aisle and one row back noticed his head jerk slightly. She watched him from the side as he pinched his eyes closed tightly and wondered if he was in pain. He'd remembered that his tuition for the next semester would soon be needed but shoved it back in his mind, unable to deal with anything more. He could feel her eyes on him and quickly turned. She held her stare but offered a weak smile, and he returned it.

A rough stretch of potholes sent the passengers bucking around in their seats. He watched as the old woman's head seemed to stagger around on her shoulders, like a little dashboard doll with its head mounted on springs. He saw her eyes open and the sudden look of panic that seized her face as she realized she was in foreign territory.

"Is this Wilshire Boulevard?" she said without looking to see who was seated next to her.

"Normandie," Junior said, leaning forward to detect just where along Normandie they were. "Normandie and 54th to be exact."

"Normandie?" Ida said, grabbing hold of her shopping bags and rising. "Missed my stop. Let me out, please?"

Junior stood and watched as Ida slid past him and began to stagger up the aisle. She stopped to try and pull the buzzer cord, but she was too short to reach over the other riders. When she reached the bus driver, she heard the buzzer being pulled by someone else.

"I missed my stop," she blurted out.

The driver looked up unconcerned and then back to the road.

"I have to get back to Wilshire Boulevard. Did you hear me?"

"Next stop," he said.

Junior made his way down the aisle to join the line of six others getting off behind Ida. The bus pulled to the curb, the hydraulic brakes hissing, and the doors opened.

"What number do I need to get back to Wilshire?" Ida asked.

"Take number seventeen, across the street," he mumbled.

The other passengers grew impatient and began pushing Ida forward and down the steps. "Seventy," she repeated, having misunderstood him. "Number seventy."

The moment Ida's feet hit the pavement, she was propelled forward and out of the way by the other riders. She sighed heavily and made her way to the traffic light. She rested the bags on the sidewalk as she waited for the light to change. "Seventy," she repeated nervously and looked down to see that her feet had swollen, pressing over the tops of her shoes. She wished she were home.

When the light changed, she stooped to lift the bags and was once again propelled forward against her will by a large black woman. Ida stumbled and was about to fall when she felt a strong hand catch her by the elbow. She looked over to see Junior standing next to her.

"Whoa. Steady, now," he said to her in a calming voice.

"Thank you. I guess I'm too slow for everyone."

"World's in a hurry. I'll help you get across," he said, guiding her toward the opposite side. Ida wobbled back and forth as she tried to step lightly on her painful feet. She felt like an old woman, something she seldom admitted to herself, and was slightly embarrassed having it happen in front of this nice young man.

"Catching the bus back?" Junior said.

"Yes. Missed my transfer point. I must have dozed off."

"I know. I was sitting next to you," Junior said, offering a reassuring smile.

"You were, weren't you?"

Junior walked Ida to the bus bench and watched as she took a seat. She looked exhausted.

"Okay now?" he asked.

"Yes. Thank you. What's your name?"

"Junior. Junior Thomas."

"Junior to who?"

"Whom. Junior to whom?"

"I stand... rather, I sit corrected. To whom are you Junior?"

"No one. Name's just Junior."

"Oh. I see," she said, even though she didn't understand. "Well, thank you for helping me, Junior."

Junior nodded, watching Ida survey the location. She still looked confused.

"Where are we again?"

"Florence and Normandie. South Central," he said, and he watched her eyes widen noticeably.

"Not 'the' Florence and Normandie?"

"Yup. But don't panic. We never riot during religious holidays, lady."

"Ida. The name is Ida, and I wasn't about to panic. I merely find it fascinating," she said. Looking around, Ida thought that it looked like any other busy corner in Los Angeles. "Seems peaceful enough, more ordinary than I'd pictured it."

"Don't let that fool you. You best watch that purse. And I'd turn that ring around if I were you."

Ida looked down at her hand and back to Junior. "Really?" she asked even as she began turning the stone inward.

"Really. Catch the first bus. You hear?" he said.

Junior turned and started to walk away.

"Merry Christmas, Junior Thomas," Ida said loudly, turning the ring back around on her finger.

Junior glanced back at her over his shoulder. "Yeah. Sure. Merry Christmas," he said, and he walked on.

Ida opened her purse and took out a Kleenex. There was a good deal of wind, both natural and traffic-made. She set her purse down next to her on the bench and blew her nose. She could smell Mexican food being cooked somewhere nearby.

She could feel that her toes were getting numb, and she lifted her right foot to take off her shoe but thought better of it. She feared that once off she would never be able to get it back on again. "Junior?" she said to herself, thinking it odd that someone would give their son such a vague name. "An adjective?" She glanced down at her watch and was surprised to see it was nearly six. Madeline would be furious with her, she thought. Where is that bus?

A number seventeen bus pulled up at the bench and several people clambered off. Most of them dispersed, but one young Mexican woman took a seat next to Ida.

"Merry Christmas," said Ida.

Maria Mendoza gave her a leery look. Her face was tight, and Ida thought she must have a headache or was perhaps worried about something. Despite the sunglasses the woman wore, Ida could see from the side that her eyes were swollen.

"Yeah," Maria mumbled in return.

"Are you waiting for a number seventy, too?" asked Ida.

"No," came her terse reply.

"Wouldn't know how often it comes by, would you?"

"No," replied Maria, as she glanced down to see Ida's purse sitting between them and the large diamond ring on her finger.

"Missed my stop. Trying to get back to Wilshire Boulevard," Ida continued.

"Yeah. Bet you are."

They sat quietly for a few moments, and Ida didn't notice the woman's eyes darting down from time to time to survey her purse.

Maria studied Ida from the corner of her eye, seeing a faint resemblance to Ruth in her size and coloring. She saw Ruth, saw all of the lucky ones who knew what they would be doing tomorrow, saw the diamond ring and the purse.

A number twenty-three bus pulled to the curb, and Maria got up to board it. Shooting one hand out to point down the street in the opposite direction, she said, "Maybe that's your bus?" When Ida turned to look, Maria scooped up Ida's purse and quickly boarded the bus.

Ida strained to see what she had pointed at but saw no bus. When she turned back the woman was gone. Looking up as the bus pulled away, she saw the woman making her way down the aisle. She had pulled off her sunglasses and wore a pained expression on her face. What Ida couldn't see was the knot in Maria's stomach, tight as a clenched fist. Nor did she experience the surge of bile that had Maria swallowing hard trying not to throw up. When Ida looked down at the bench, she realized her purse had been taken. She knew immediately why the woman had looked so troubled. Ida's heart sunk, and her eyes squeezed shut.

"Don't panic," she whispered to herself. She remembered Junior's advice about watching her purse. Her hand instinctively felt for the stone on her ring. It was safely there, and she turned it under once again, this time leaving it there. What did it really matter? she thought. It was a few hundred dollars at the most, her one and only credit card which she could stop when she got home, some old cosmetics and a package of gum. She must have been desperate and the thought made Ida sad. She wouldn't call the police. It would only delay her getting home.

Her eyes popped wide as she realized she had no money, though. Then the transfer ticket screamed to her from her pocket. She reached in and pulled it out. Safe, she thought. I can still get home.

She leaned down and pulled the shopping bags in underneath her legs, determined to follow Junior's advice with what was left.

CHAPTER TEN

Junior saw Mr. Raymond leaving the building as he approached. It wasn't often their landlord set foot on his property. He kept a low profile, choosing to distance himself from any possible tenant complaints about the rundown condition of the building. He approached Mr. Raymond with some caution, hoping Queen really had paid the rent.

"Evening, Mr. Raymond," he said, offering a smile.

"She ain't paid me my rent money, Junior. Miss Eula said she did, but 'tain't so," Mr. Raymond's chubby cheeks puffed out the slaughtered verbs. Junior didn't try to correct him.

"She didn't?" Junior said, trying to look surprised.

"Got to have my rents."

"Yes, of course. I'll... I'll check it out with Queen, Mr. Raymond. You'll get paid. I promise."

"Monday, you hear? People's got bills to pay. Can't be waitin' 'round for long."

"You'll have it. I'll see to it."

Mr. Raymond frowned down over his wire-rimmed bifocals in an effort to drive the point home. He mustered a weak smile then and asked, "Miss Eula looks tired, Junior?"

"Yeah. Her arthritis has been pretty bad. She gets worn down."

"Take care of her, you hear?" he said as he walked down the street, not waiting for Junior's reply.

Junior pushed through the double door entrance to the apartment building, running headlong into their neighbor Alvin Burke.

"Whoa, Junior. Slow down."

"Sorry, Mr. Burke."

"Miss Eula didn't come by for coffee. She not feeling good?"

"Arthritis is acting up."

"Too bad," he said, shaking his withered head. "She tells me you're gonna be a doctor, Junior. That so?"

"Maybe. It'll be awhile, though. I can only go part time right now. But maybe," Junior said, moving backward down the hall, trying to escape.

"Maybe you'll win the lottery."

"Can't afford to play."

Junior entered the apartment to find his grandmother shuffling down the hallway to her room. "Home, Gramma," he said, stopping her journey.

"Oh, Junior, we got problems."

"I know. I saw Mr. Raymond out front."

"Don't say it. I know you warned me," she said in a low voice.

"Is she home?"

"No. Went out earlier. Had an appointment."

Junior spotted the folded note stuck in the warped frame of the mahogany mirror over the hall table, "Mamma" scratched in large shaky letters across its face. He knew immediately what it would say. He sighed heavily, thinking how the note would hurt his grandmother. He reached over and plucked it from the frame.

"Have you seen this?" he said, holding the note up.

"No. What is it?"

Junior unfolded the note, recognizing Queen's scrawl. He read the tersely written four lines and gulped back his own revulsion. He looked up from the note to see his grandmother headed his way.

"Dammit!" he yelled, knowing his grandmother wouldn't like it. He looked up suddenly and his eyes widened. He ran past Eula and into what had been his bedroom. Throwing open the closet door, he reached up on the shelf and pulled down the coffee can. He closed his eyes as he removed the lid, hoping she hadn't. When he looked, sure enough, the money was gone.

The coffee can hit the wall just as Eula rounded the doorway. Startled, she backed up a few feet, the can rolling along the floor as if to follow her.

"What on earth?"

"Damn her! Damn her all to hell!"

"Junior!"

"The phone money. The rent money. Even your Christmas present money. She's run off with it all, Gramma."

"Run off?"

Junior waved the note. "She's gone. Says she's sorry, but she has to leave," he hesitated. "I hope she dies. I hope she overdoses."

"Junior! Don't... don't say such things. You don't mean that."

"Yes, I do. I swear I do."

Eula walked to his side and took the note. She read it carefully, her eyes squinting to make out Queen's hand. She felt a knot growing inside her stomach and her shoulders slumped forward. When she was through, she sat down on Junior's bed.

"We've got to stop her, Junior."

"Stop her?"

"Yes. We've got to catch up with her before she gets too far."

"I'm not stopping her. I hope she rots in hell."

"Stop that!" Eula said in a voice so strong it frightened Junior.

"But Gramma, we have no money," he pleaded with her. "You realize that. We have no money to pay the rent."

"I said stop. We have got to find her. I got a bad feeling about this. You read the note. She's at the end. Says she's taking a big chance."

"She's long gone by now."

"Maybe, but we have to try. I want you to look for her."

"Let her go. Good riddance."

"I know!" she said, straightening her shoulders and opening her eyes wide. "Go see that Mr. Aziz at the liquor store. He may know something. She likes Mr. Aziz. Maybe she went by?"

"Don't make me chase after her, Gramma."

"Please, Junior. I'm asking, please. See Mr. Aziz?"

"But your birthday present..." he began; he saw her eyes and gave in. "Oh, all right! For you, though, not for her, for you."

CHAPTER ELEVEN

The glare of the neon sign in front of *Custom Wine and Spirits* could be seen for blocks. Surrounding the neon, a raceway of clear light bulbs seemed to roll, directing the eye around the square sign by blinking in order, ending in a giant arrow that pointed to the entrance. Junior slowly approached, wishing he hadn't promised his grandmother he'd ask Mr. Aziz about Queen. It was bad enough that the whole neighborhood knew what she was, now they'd know she'd run off again. He had half a notion not to ask, but he couldn't bring himself to let his grandmother down. And there was no way he would lie to her.

As he walked up the sidewalk leading to the front door, he saw Ida sitting on the bus bench where he'd left her forty-five minutes ago. The lines that appeared on his forehead told of his concern for the old woman. Why wasn't she home by now? It was enough of a distraction to change his direction.

With her back to Junior, Ida didn't see him approach nor could she hear the footfalls of his tennis shoes. As a result, she jumped when she heard his voice. "Still here?" he said, rounding the bench to stand next to her.

When she saw who it was, Ida closed her eyes and gave an audible sigh of relief.

"You scared me," she said, gathering her composure. "No number seventy bus has come by yet."

"Seventy? There's no seventy on this route. Forty one, twenty three and seventeen, but no seventy."

"Really?"

"Yeah. If you're going north, you need a number seventeen."

"No wonder," she said, mustering a halfhearted laugh.

Junior's eyes scanned the emptiness of bench beside Ida, "Where's your purse?"

Ida avoided Junior's stare as she admitted, "A lady picked it up... by mistake, though."

"By mistake? Nobody picks up a purse by mistake."

"She did. She was in a hurry to board her bus. I'm sure she'll realize it later and get it back to me."

"She stole your purse."

"No. No, I'm sure it was a mistake."

Junior shook his head. "Lady, you're a fool. She stole your purse, face it."

"Ida. My name is Ida, and I'm no fool."

"This isn't Beverly Hills, Ida. She stole your purse. Want me to call the police?"

"No, thank you. She'll get it back to me."

"Yeah. Well, how are you going to get home with no money?"

Ida fished the transfer ticket from her pocket and held it up. "With this."

"Okay. Take the next number seventeen and watch those bags," he said, looking down at her hand to make sure the diamond was not exposed. "And don't talk to anyone."

"I'm perfectly safe. God will watch over me."

"Maybe. Just be sure and catch the next bus."

"I will," Ida said as Junior walked away. "Junior,"

she called.

Junior turned to look back, "Yes?"

"Thank you, again. That's twice you've helped me."

Junior smiled and continued on to the liquor store. He looked back at Ida as he pushed open the grimy glass door and shook his head. Like Gramma, he thought.

The counter was vacant as Junior approached. Somewhere in the store Mr. Aziz burned incense, a sweet, noxious odor Junior found repugnant. His eyes caught a display of brightly packaged condoms of various types. He wondered if this was where Queen got her supply. He knew she bought pint bottles of cheap vodka here.

Over the far edge of the counter, he saw the top of Mr. Aziz's bald head. There was a three-inch crease in his scalp from the bullet fired by a robber three years ago. Mr. Aziz was stuffing a large stack of 20s and 50s into a crumpled brown paper bag. Junior watched as he stuffed the bag behind the safe bolted to the cabinet floor instead of inside it and closed the door, having given up on locking anything of value inside the safe itself after so many robberies.

"Ahem," Junior cleared his voice to get his attention.

Mr. Aziz whirled around on his haunches, his eyes large and white against his swarthy complexion. He looked terrorized.

"Excuse me, Mr. Aziz."

"Junior," he said, heaving a noticeable sigh of relief. "You startled me." There was a musical quality to his voice that fascinated Junior. It was more East Indian than Arab because Mr. Aziz had lived in Delhi before moving to Los Angeles. Before that, he had lived and gone to school in London, so he spoke very proper English. Junior liked Mr. Aziz.

"Sorry. Have you seen Queen, Mr. Aziz?"

The little man rose to his feet, absentmindedly

smoothing back what was left of the hair on each side of his head. "Not since yesterday. Cato was here looking for her, too."

"When was that?"

"Half an hour ago. What's the matter?"

"She's run off again."

"Cato was so very mad, Junior."

"No doubt. Can't make any money with one of his girls off the street."

Mr. Aziz looked down shyly. "I'm sure I wouldn't know anything about that, Junior."

"Then you're the only one around here who doesn't," Junior said, knowing that Mr. Aziz was too much of a gentleman to discuss such a subject let alone acknowledge his awareness of it.

A scream interrupted their conversation. Junior turned to see that the door had not closed behind him. He heard a second scream, a woman's voice yelling, "Help!" Without thinking, Junior ran out of the store. Looking toward the bus bench, he saw a low-slung, green Honda with its lights on sitting by the curb with its front door open wide. Rap music boomed from inside the car. He saw Ida struggling to hold onto her shopping bags as a young Latino pulled in the opposite direction. Junior took off running across the parking lot as the youth raised one hand and knocked Ida to the ground with his fist.

"Hey! Hey, you! Stop!" Junior yelled as he ran.

Before he could reach the bench, the Latino had jumped into the front seat. He heard the squeal of the little car's tires and could smell the burning rubber and exhaust as he reached the edge of the bench. The car was already half a block away.

Junior knelt down next to Ida. He could see blood on the side of her head where her earring must have taken the blow, cutting deeply into the scalp behind her right ear. She was unconscious. He lifted her head slightly to get a better look. Ida moaned.

Mr. Aziz bent down next to Junior. "Is she all right?"

"Took a bad fall. He hit her in the head."

"I'll call an ambulance and the police," Mr. Aziz said, rising quickly and scurrying away.

"Oh-h-h-h," Ida moaned as she regained consciousness.

"Sh-h-h-h. Stay still. You've been hurt," Junior said as Ida opened one eye. He smiled at her and eased her head back to the sidewalk. "Be still, now. Help is coming."

"Junior? You again," Ida said in a weak voice. "They took my presents. My son's sweater."

"Sh-h-h-h," he said, as Ida blacked out again.

~*~

It was an unearthly wail, ceaseless, relentless. Why wouldn't it stop, she thought, rolling her head and squeezing her eyelids tight against the noise. Junior silently watched her unconscious, restless motions, wondering what it was she imagined. Her hand reached out to stop the ringing, as if her alarm clock was nearby and its source.

He took her pale-white trembling hand in his as the ambulance turned into the driveway of Martin Luther King, Jr. Memorial Hospital. He watched the row of palm trees through the rear window until the first of them rapidly became the focal point two hundred yards away as the ambulance came to a stop. The siren petered out slowly, leaving a dead silence in its wake and only the red lights to circle the ambulance and bounce off the glass doors of the hospital.

With the siren's silencing, Ida mumbled, "Thank you, Madeline," without opening her eyes and she squeezed Junior's hand. He cocked his head and gave her a quizzical look. Who was Madeline, and why was she being thanked?

The attendants pulled open the rear doors and offered Junior a hand in exiting. He watched them pull the stretcher halfway out, stopping to extend the first set of chrome legs and then pulling it a little farther for the second set. Instant gurney, he thought. Cool. As they jockeyed the gurney around, he saw Ida's eyes open. They were wide with alarm, the same look he'd seen on her face when she awoke on the bus earlier in the evening.

"What? What?" she mumbled softly, rolling her head to survey her strange surroundings. The flashing red lights circling above her furthered her confusion and added to her panic. "What's happening?"

Junior snatched her hand, stopping it from trying to feel the red flashes in the air. He leaned closer as the gurney began moving toward the emergency room entrance so Ida could see his face. He smiled and Ida's eyes seemed to wilt with relief. "It's okay. I'm here." Ida smiled.

The smell was more herbal than medicinal, perhaps a pine-based cleaner, as they rolled into the emergency room, making a sharp right hand turn, passing two rows of what he assumed to be relatives or the more minor injured of the patients. He barely saw them, but he noted that not one was white save Ida. His tennis shoes squeaked on the highly polished terrazzo floors as they proceeded down another hallway.

They came to a stop outside two chrome-plated swinging doors. A heavyset black nurse leaned over to look at the side of Ida's head, using one large black hand to push back the stray gray hairs. She smiled broadly at Ida, asking, "Know where you are, sugar?"

"If this isn't a hospital, I'm in deep trouble," Ida said, the fresh air having restored her.

The nurse chuckled. "You and me both," she said, turning her attention to Junior. "Who are you?" she said in a suddenly gruff voice.

"Grandson," he lied, knowing anything less would exclude him.

"Take her to number seven," she ordered the attendants.

With a loud set of bumps, the two doors flew open as the attendants used the gurney as a battering ram. Junior started to follow, but the big nurse stepped in front of him, hands on hips and elbows extended. She had a mean look on her face.

"Grandson my ass," she said frowning, her almost black face coming inches from his light brown one. Junior must have look startled because she dropped her head and peered over her wire-rimmed glasses. He gave her his most pleading look, saying nothing. They stared at each other as the nurse sized him up. With a shrug, she tossed her head toward the doors and said, "Go ahead."

"Thank you," he said, inching around her large frame as if she were the pivot point of his radius.

When Junior reached room number seven, two Filipino nurses had already transferred Ida to a bed and the ambulance attendants were retreating with their gurney. One nurse was filling out a form, asking Ida pertinent data. Ida looked up and, seeing Junior, extended her hand to him. He walked over to the side of the bed and took it in his.

"That's three times," she said, giving him a weak smile and squeezing his hand tightly in hers.

"Maybe you need a keeper."

"God sent you, Junior."

"Yeah? Sure," he said with a frown of disbelief.

"Thank you for coming with me."

"Had no choice. You wouldn't let go of my hand," Junior said with a laugh.

A darkly beautiful young woman dressed in the light-green pajamas of a doctor entered. She was East Indian and a stethoscope hung around her neck. Her silky black hair had been braided and drawn up into two neat bundles on either side of her head behind her ears. Junior wondered how long it was. The nurse with the information clipboard handed it to her and she quickly reviewed it.

"Are you a doctor?" Ida asked.

"Dr. Dogra, Mrs. Hanson. How is your vision?" she asked without responding to the surprised look on Ida's face. She was used to skeptical looks, knowing that her youthful appearance, gender, and nationality created obstacles for some.

"Fine. Just fine," Ida said.

"No double vision? Dizziness? Shortness of breath?"

"No, I have a headache. That's all."

The doctor took a chrome penlight from her coat pocket and trained the light into Ida's eyes one at a time. She raised her other hand in front of Ida's face. "Follow my hand with both eyes, Mrs. Hanson," she ordered. Ida did as she was told.

Junior moved to the end of the bed, watching Dr. Dogra carefully. He was fascinated and longed to ask questions about what she was watching for, what signs were indicative of what damage.

"Is my voice clear to you, Mrs. Hanson?"

Ida looked puzzled for a moment. "Your English is perfect," she said.

Dr. Dogra smiled knowingly. "No. That's not what I meant, but thank you. I mean. Do you hear echoes when I speak? Any ringing?"

"Oh. Yes. I mean. No. No echoes or ringing. My hearing is fine."

"Good," she said, switching off the penlight and returning it to her pocket. She lifted Ida's right arm and pinched along the bones from wrist to armpit. She did the same with the other arm and then asked Ida to lift one leg at a time and flex her knees. "Good," she said again.

Turning to the rolling cart left by one of the nurses, Dr. Dogra lifted the chrome lid on a glass cylinder and set the jar and lid on the bedside table. She withdrew a cotton ball and a patch of gauze, wrapping the gauze around the little ball. She opened a bottle of clear liquid and soaked the gauzed cotton. With one swarthy hand, she lifted Ida's pale head by her chin. Junior noticed a series of dark purple tattoos across the first joint of each of her fingers just below the knuckle and wondered what exotic ritual they spoke of and what the symbols represented. Turning Ida's head to the side, she said, "This may sting a bit," and she began to gently dab the wound. Ida flinched and squeezed her eyes shut. The smell of alcohol cleansed the air in the room. "Well, I'd say you've been very lucky. I do want X-rays, though. Just to be sure," she said. Junior thought it odd that there was no trace of an accent in the Doctor's voice.

"Take her to X-ray and let me know when they're through," Dr. Dogra instructed the nurse. "I'll see you in a few minutes, Mrs. Hanson," she said as she walked out the door.

The nurse asked Ida if she felt she could walk, and Ida told her she not only could but that she preferred it. Ida got down off the bed and the nurse took her arm. Ida turned to Junior before leaving, "Will your mother be worried about you?"

"Queen? Worry? No way. Probably shooting up somewhere."

"Shooting up?" Ida said, stopping suddenly.

"Dope. Heroin, most likely."

Ida's mouth dropped open slightly in amazement and the little nurse turned her head away, pretending not to have heard him.

"That shock you?" Junior said matter-of-factly.

"Shock me? Yes. Yes, that shocks me. I... I'm sorry."

Junior shrugged. "Don't be. I'm used to it," he said, smiling weakly at Ida. "That's what God does down my way."

Ida shook her head. "God doesn't do that, Junior," she said, wanting to reach out and touch him.

"Oh, yeah. Sure about that, huh?"

"Absolutely... Will you wait for me, then?" she said, giving him a worried look.

"Sure. I'll wait. Don't worry."

CHAPTER TWELVE

At 8:00 p.m., Madeline sat at the kitchen table playing Solitaire and worrying. After Ida'd left that morning and her pie was safely cooling on a rack in the kitchen, Madeline had spent the rest of the day playing the piano. The piano was Madeline's church and music her religion. It had been that way since the day she started playing for the church choir when Mrs. Thornton failed to show up for the service, having died quietly in her sleep. Madeline was twelve at the time and the only other member of the church who could play a piano. And she played quite competently thanks to her mother, who had insisted that each of her five children learn to play a musical instrument. The fact that they did not own nor could they afford a piano hadn't stopped her mother. From the age of seven, Madeline had taken lessons twice a week from Mrs. Thornton using the church's piano and had practiced on it every Saturday afternoon.

And so, it had seemed a fitting way to spend the day. A bit of revenge for being left behind? Perhaps. But to Madeline, it was more the freedom it afforded her being alone in the old house, a golden opportunity. She could play as loud as she liked and play what she liked, no interruptions, no special requests, just Madeline sitting in her church practicing her religion. And that's what she'd done straight through until 4:30 when she looked up and realized it was time to start dinner.

When 5:30 rolled around, Madeline began to worry about Ida, and by 7:30 she was frantic. Twice she had walked to the curb, staring down the street, holding one hand over her eyes against the occasional slits of the setting sun through the overcast sky. She could see all the way to Wilshire Boulevard, but no Ida. Both times she'd left the front door propped open in case the phone rang. But it never did. She had called every hospital in the area and the police twice, but still no Ida.

Madeline's hand was shaking as she attempted to put the nine of hearts on the ten of spades, and in doing so, she disrupted the longer row of cards on the left. In a fit of angst, she swept the cards off the table onto the kitchen floor, toppling her glass of iced tea in the process. "Where is she?" she growled as she watched the stream of liquid spread across the table, the ice having melted long ago.

For the first time in all the years she'd lived in the house, she realized that she could hear the ticking of the grandfather's clock in the front hall. She'd never noticed it before in the kitchen, the hall but not the kitchen. It struck her too that, while it was a quiet house with just the two of them occupying it for most of the past thirty years, she had never found it lonely. But it was lonely now. Quiet and empty.

"Where is she?" she repeated aloud. She hadn't been this anxious since, since when? Years and years, Madeline thought. A frown formed as she recalled just when. Her seventeenth birthday. And she could still picture herself sitting on the front porch of their little clapboard house in Peoria dressed in her blue-and-white polka dot dress and white-straw Sunday hat. She wore her best white low-heeled pumps, which she'd polished for the big trip. She was sitting and waiting for him to come and take her away. Her cardboard suitcase hidden beneath the worn wooden steps, out of her mother's sight should she return before he came for her, the note written to her mother resting against the toaster on the kitchen counter.

Oh Lord, she thought to herself, shaking her head. You need to let go of that. It wasn't often she thought of him, but when she did, she still experienced the churning in her stomach and a profound disappointment. But she could still see him. Tall and suave and dressed so fancy, he had been everything the young men of her small circle were not, worldly, dangerous.

His name was Billy Lee, the big city cousin of her best friend Sukie, and he'd come from Chicago to spend the summer. He talked of train trips to New Orleans and New York to catch the newest bands. He looked older than nineteen, talked older than nineteen, and he'd been to nightclubs and speakeasies, or so he claimed. He played duets on the piano with her and taught her the latest tunes, singing ragtime sometimes or moodily swaying to jazz in the empty church. And it was there on a creaking pew that she had given in to him, or he to her. It didn't matter. It was something she'd wanted just as much as he did. And he was taking her away. She had told Sukie but no one else.

She remembered sitting patiently waiting and hoping that he would come before her mother returned from the dinner party at the Romans, the old couple she cooked and cleaned for each day. She had worried what her mother's reaction would be. Would she find the note that night or the next morning, having gone straight to bed after a fourteen-hour day?

In the end, he never came for her. He'd taken the train hours earlier, leaving her to sit on the porch and wait. It was Sukie who finally came to tell her. And it was Sukie who waved good-bye to her when she boarded a train for Los Angeles the next day. He may have left without her, but she wouldn't be left behind. She couldn't sit in Peoria waiting and hoping he'd come back for her, and she knew that was what would happen. She didn't want every train whistle catching her attention, and it would. She knew it would.

Enough, she thought. Enough of that stuff.

She looked up at the clock to see that it was 8:30. She slumped forward, placing one elbow in the pool of spilt tea without noticing it and rested her head in her hand. "She's dead," she whispered, thinking now what am I to do? Ida was Madeline's only friend. Ida was all she had in the world. Her mother was gone, her three brothers had been killed in Korea and her little sister had died at the age of three. She had never known who her father was. "You can't do this to me," she said, getting up to fetch the towel and returning to wipe up the tea. "Please don't."

Stooping to the floor, she began to pick up the cards, regretting having made the mess. She thought about calling the morgue, about how long she should wait to call the hospitals and police again. When she'd gathered the cards, she rose and slid them back into the box.

Unable to sit any longer, she went back into the front hall and opened the door, noticing that the handle was already getting loose. The cold night air seemed oddly thick with the heady scent of the star jasmine that grew along the driveway. She stared out into the darkness. The house was quiet. The street was deserted. She couldn't make up her mind whether to go out and sit on the steps or go back in. She leaned against the door frame, turning so that she could see both inside and out. Loneliness on both sides, Madeline thought, no way to turn.

She glanced over to see the silver-framed picture of

Ida's son sitting on the hall table. "Is this ours now?" she said to Donald, knowing that everything Ida owned had been left to him and, failing his return, to her. "Hope not," she whispered, knowing he'd never be coming home.

~*~

Shortly after Ida returned to the room, Dr. Dogra came in holding a set of X-rays. Junior watched as she switched on a lighted box hanging on the wall, and he drew closer for a better look. She studied them carefully, turning suddenly to find herself nose-to-nose with Junior.

"Wonder what I'm looking for?" she said.

"Yeah."

She turned back to the X-rays and pointed out the area of Ida's skull that had sustained the blow. "See this? We look for hairline fractures." She moved her finger down the X-ray. "Also, any dislocation of the jaw or spreading of gaps near or within bone mass." She moved to the other X-rays of Ida's torso and appendages. "Alignment. That sort of thing," she said as he watched her finger trace the lighter areas of the film.

Junior was mesmerized. Dr. Dogra watched him with interest, not turning her head but looking from the corner of her dark eyes. "Interested in medicine?" she said, smiling for the first time as she continued to study the X-ray.

"Very," he said, turning to look at her. "I'd like to study medicine," he admitted.

"Hello," Ida interrupted from her chair in the corner, anxious to hear the outcome.

The doctor walked over to Ida and looked down. "X-rays show no damage, Mrs. Hanson. You'll be very sore tomorrow. But if you are feeling all right, I see no reason to keep you. I think you'll rest easier at home."

"Good," Ida sighed in relief.

"You're a lucky woman," the doctor added.

"God watches over me."

"Got a damn funny way of doing it," said Junior, shaking his head.

Dr. Dogra eyed them both carefully, wondering what was their connection but too polite to ask. She withdrew a vial of pills from her pocket and handed it to Ida. "Take two when you get home. Two every four hours for pain. I'd see your family physician tomorrow if I were you."

"Thank you, Doctor."

~*~

It was 8:30 when Ida and Junior walked out of the hospital and a cold breeze greeted them. One panel of Ida's coat blew open and she pulled it back into place, buttoning it against the wind. She noticed for the first time that Junior was not wearing a coat, and she envied his youthful resilience. She reached up to feel her hair, which she knew must be crushed against her head after the ambulance ride and hospital bed. She tried to fluff it a bit, but to no avail. She felt messy.

She took Junior's arm, and remembering his conversation with Dr. Dogra, she said, "So you want to be a doctor?"

"Yes. Well, maybe." Then he remembered his current troubles and with a frown said, "Maybe not."

"You should meet my son. He's a doctor, too. You'd like him."

"Yeah? Cool."

"Thank you for all your help, Junior."

"It was nothing."

"No. It was not nothing. It was very, very kind of you. I don't know how I would have managed without your support."

"It was no problem. Really," he said. Changing the subject self-consciously, "How are you going to get home?"

Ida rummaged in her coat pocket and pulled out the bus transfer, holding it up. "This. I guess."

"No," Junior said firmly, "absolutely not. We'll flag you a cab."

"Junior, I have no purse, no money and no credit cards. Besides, I've already paid for the transfer."

A few yards away, a taxi pulled up and two nurses got out. Junior took Ida by the arm, forcefully guiding her to the cab. He pulled a twenty dollar bill from his pocket and handed it to Ida.

"No. You've done enough already. I couldn't."

"Just a loan. To get you home."

"But what about you? How will you get home?"

"Twelve blocks away. No sweat," he said, leaning down to the cab's window. "Lady needs a ride home." The driver nodded. Junior opened the door. "Please?"

"All right. On one condition," she said, twisting her diamond ring from her finger and handing it to Junior.

"What's this?"

"Security for the loan. I want you to come to my home tomorrow. I want to repay you and to thank you."

Junior shook his head and tried to hand the ring back to Ida. "Call it a Christmas present," he said. "Please?"

"Do you have a pen and a scrap of paper?" she asked the driver, ignoring Junior. The driver frowned, dug around on the front seat, and handed Ida a pencil and a flyer advertising tires at a discount. Ida flipped the paper over, quickly scratched out her address and phone number, and handed it to Junior.

"Come tomorrow," she said as she eased into the back seat, feeling the soreness settling into her hip and right arm, and closed the door.

Junior leaned down to the open window and tried to hand the ring back to Ida. "No. Really. Here. I can't take this."

Ida reached out and closed his warm brown hand around her ring. "I insist."

"Really. Just call the twenty a gift."

Ida leaned forward, holding onto the windowsill, pushing Junior's hand back. "You were my gift, Junior, and a Godsend, too. Come tomorrow?"

"Okay. If you insist," he relented with a shrug of his shoulders.

As the cab pulled away, Junior called after her. "Sorry about your son's Christmas present."

CHAPTER THIRTEEN

Junior's pace slowed dramatically as he rounded the corner of Sheldon Avenue on his way home from the hospital. He was still fascinated by the brown-black X-rays, the exotic doctor and the strangely open old woman and in no hurry to usurp their place in his thoughts. He wished he'd asked about the tattoos, about the metal pin in Ida's shoulder that appeared in the X-ray and what type of doctor her son was. It seemed as if he'd just visited another planet, stepping into a new world that he had only dreamed of before.

The headlights of a car turning onto Sheldon from behind him scanned the street ahead. He saw Cato's big white Cadillac convertible with its gaudy gold trim parked in front of his apartment building. Even the normally chrome wire wheels had been dipped in the too-bright-a-yellow faux golden plating. His eyes registered the fear that ran through his mind, bringing him back into the real world.

He broke into a run, hoping no harm had come to his grandmother. As he reached the steps in front of the apartment building, Cato walked out the door. He was tall and barrel-chested with massive arms. His shaved head reflected the light of a lamp in Mr. Johnson's window. Junior could see his eyes burning with anger even in the dim light of the single exposed bulb above the entrance. He stopped dead, unable to speak, feeling his heart rapidly pounding for freedom from the cage of his chest.

"Where's Queen, Junior?"

Hoping that he wasn't too late, Junior rushed forward trying to pass by him. But Cato grabbed a handful of Junior's sweatshirt, stopping him abruptly. "Said where's Queen, boy?"

"You didn't hurt Gramma?"

"Hurt an old lady? Get serious," Cato said, but his eyes warned against believing him. Cato twisted the sweatshirt, drawing him up and into the warm, decaying teeth smell of his breath that Junior struggled to ignore. He gagged, trying not to inhale. "Where is she, boy?"

"Gone. Left a note. Gone for good," he said, struggling to free himself. Cato's massive fist pulled his sweatshirt higher. Junior could feel the cool air on his exposed stomach.

"Where?"

"Didn't say. Vegas, probably. I don't know," he said, trembling as he spoke.

"Bitch owes me two grand, Junior. We had us an agreement this time. I warned her. I get paid or someone gets hurt. You hear?"

As Cato's eyes moved dangerously close to his, he saw that a sickly yellow surrounded his dark brown irises. "She took everything, Cato. Honest," he pleaded.

To Junior's surprise, Cato slowly untwisted his fist, easing him back down from the balls of his feet and smiled. "I got other employees, Junior," Cato said in a vaguely condescending voice. He reached out and pretended to smooth nonexistent wrinkles from Junior's sweatshirt. The feel of Cato's large hands rubbing across Junior's nipples through the thick fabric made him cringe.

"Can't be having them think nothing happens. Now can I, boy? Wouldn't want 'em gettin any ideas."

"But we have no money," Junior said, louder than necessary.

Cato lifted one finger to his lips to shush him and then directed it to Junior's chest, thumping it hard. "Someone pays. She knew the rules. Got twenty-four hours. You hear?"

Cato walked down the steps. Junior swallowed hard and called after him. "We don't have two thousand dollars."

Cato glanced back over his shoulder, "You ain't been listening, boy. I get my money or..."

"Or what?" Junior asked, his eyes narrowing, looking sad and afraid.

"Funny how old ladies is always falling down. Ain't it," Cato said, offering a sly smile. "Damn funny."

Junior was frozen in place as he watched Cato get into the car and start it. The window made a little hum as it lowered, disappearing into the door. The radio blared a rock song, shattering the silence along the narrow dark street.

"Twenty-four hours," he said over the radio's noise, and he pulled away from the curb slowly, his face drawing up in a false, closed-lipped grin.

Junior watched as the red taillights slowly floated down the street and rounded the corner onto Slauson. Defeated, he sighed and turned to enter the building, wondering what Cato had said to his grandmother.

Eula was sitting in the living room when he walked in. She looked up, asking "You find her?" but her tone said she already knew the answer. Her eyes were all sadness and worry.

Junior shook his head slowly, watching her slump at his unspoken answer. "You okay, Gramma?"

"Yes. Yes, I suppose," she said, working her hands,

alternately squeezing them as if she were battling the cold. "A man was here. He was looking for Mae. Said she owes him money."

"Name's Cato," Junior said.

"I know," she said, turning away from him, realizing for the first time that Junior knew who Cato was.

"He's Queen's pimp," Junior said, wanting her to realize the danger, knowing she wouldn't like his saying it.

She slowly turned her head back to face Junior, looking at him through lifeless eyes. "I know that, too," she said softly with no sign of emotion, as if numbed by a loved one's death. She wondered how much more he knew about Cato.

The look pierced Junior, stabbing directly into his heart. He felt his lower lip quiver and found his eyes welling up with tears. It became difficult to breathe through the moisture forming in his nasal passages. He sniffled, hoping the tears would not roll down his cheeks, but one did, and he turned slightly to the left to hide it from his grandmother. With one casual stroke, he flattened the teardrop against his cheek with the palm of his left hand and continued the motion up and back through his hair and down the back of his neck. He hated Queen for having done this to her.

"He wants two thousand within twenty-four hours," he said, snorting back the mucus, wishing he had a handkerchief. "Probably money from the johns. Maybe drug money."

"I don't want to hear that," she said, looking away again.

"You have to," he said, his voice suddenly raising for emphasis. "This is serious. She's a prostitute and a drug addict. She stole from Cato, from me. Took our rent."

Eula stood, pulling her shoulders back, lifting her head as if proud in spite of what had happened and said, "She's still my baby. My... baby. I don't have to listen to that. You hear me?"

Junior shook his head. "Okay. All right. But we got big trouble here. We need money."

"There's four hundred under my mattress. Under my mattress just in case," she said, starting to walk toward the hallway.

"That's not enough. The rent alone is six hundred," he said, shoving his hand deep into the pockets of his jeans in frustration. Ida's ring took the fingers of his right hand by surprise. He had completely forgotten about it, and he rolled it between them, feeling the diamond's hardness. He pulled it out slowly and held it to the light. He chewed at the right side of his lower lip, staring into the multicolored facets, seeing in his mind Ida smiling from the window of the cab.

"What's that?" Eula said, squinting at the twinkling object in his hand.

He was sick to his stomach and had a difficult time swallowing as he held up the ring. "The answer... maybe."

~*~

With each turn the cab made, Ida winced in pain, unable to keep her body from shifting on the slick vinyl seat. When it finally turned left onto Wilshire Boulevard, Ida managed a smile. She wanted to be home and tucked into her warm bed, and she knew she was getting close. She'd asked the driver to roll up his window, finding the night air frigid and damp, but he said he needed the air to stay alert. He had rolled it up halfway after making his point, but she was still cold.

She reached into her pocket and removed the small vial of pills, noticing Dr. Dogra's name and remembering how Junior had been so taken with the X-rays. She couldn't help but think of her own son's love for anything medical, how he would talk for hours about what he was studying and how proud she'd been when he graduated from UCLA Medical School. And she wondered if Junior would be able to do the same. Had he been serious about his mother's addiction? She hoped not. It was a world she knew little about, but she knew one thing. Junior was a special person, and special people find a way.

After the driver turned the cab onto Hudson, she settled back into the seat, letting the arms relax that had braced her against sideways movement. "Almost home," she whispered to herself. As they pulled to the curb, she saw Madeline seated on the threshold of the open front door, the porch light catching her normally neatly combed hair. Ida saw the clumps of hair standing out from the side of her head and realized just how much worry she'd caused.

She paid the driver and opened the door, watching Madeline stand to place her hands firmly on her hips. She tucked the pills into her coat pocket, stepped out and slammed the door. She was determined to walk as normal as she possibly could.

CHAPTER FOURTEEN

Madeline walked cautiously down the hallway, watching the orange juice slosh hazardously in the tall glass. Even though she'd purposely under-filled it, allowing it a little room to play but not enough to spill over the edge, she kept a close eye on the contents. Her feet shuffled along the worn central path of the ancient Oriental runner, the wooden floor below creaking occasionally. When she reached Ida's door, she balanced the tray in one hand, fumbling to find the doorknob hidden beneath it.

"What's this?" Ida said, seeing her enter with the tray. She tried to sound irritated at being served breakfast in bed, which she secretly hoped would happen when she woke earlier to the smell of bacon frying and bread toasting.

"Breakfast," Madeline said, crossing the room, "but don't go getting used to it."

"Heaven forbid I should be waited on."

Madeline watched Ida wince as she sat up in bed, positioning two pillows behind her and folding the covers down over her lap. Madeline placed the tray in front of her and unfolded a white linen napkin, handing it to her.

"What, no flower? I don't rate a flower?"

Madeline ignored her and set about opening the heavy velvet drapes. Bright sunlight flooded the room. "How's the head this morning?"

"Hurts like hell," Ida said, picking up a stiff strip of bacon and biting off a small piece.

Madeline picked up the bottle of pills sitting on the night stand and read the label. "Two every four hours for pain. You take two already?"

"No."

"Last night? You took two when you went to bed, right?"

"No," Ida said, avoiding Madeline's eyes and continuing to chew on the bacon.

"You're so damn stubborn," she said, opening the bottle and shaking out two of the tablets. She handed them to Ida, shaking her hand in front of her face to get her attention. "Here! Now!" Madeline barked. Ida took the pills in her hand and curled one side of her upper lip at Madeline.

"You're so damn bossy," Ida said as she lifted the glass and pretended to pop the pills into her mouth.

"Now, you eat every bite of this. Gonna need it."

"Eat every bite of this," Ida said mockingly, shaking her head. She watched as Madeline picked up the dress she'd left lying on the chair and opened the closet to hang it up. She reached around quickly, tucking the pills under her pillow.

"Staying in bed today, too," Madeline said as she closed the closet door.

"Am not."

"Am too."

"Am not," Ida grumped. "Junior is coming by. Don't want him to worry."

"Ha! Coming by, indeed. You've seen the last of that boy, not to mention a certain ring."

"I have not."

Madeline walked to the side of Ida's bed. She reached down quickly, shoving her hand under the pillow to withdraw the hidden pills, having caught a glimpse of Ida's attempt to avoid taking them in the vanity mirror. She handed them to Ida and crossed her arms, resolving to wait until Ida had taken them.

Ida stuck her tongue out at her, but dutifully swallowed the pills, washing them down with a gulp of juice. She lifted her empty hands to prove it, giving Madeline a forced smile.

"And the last of that purse, too. Nothing but gangs down there. Gangs and welfare cheats."

"How would you know? You've never been down there. Moved in here with me straight from Peoria."

"Don't have to go to know."

"Never been south of Pico Boulevard, have you?"

"Trash. Nothing but trash," Madeline said, walking around the bed to the other window and pulling back the drapes.

Ida watched to see if Madeline's jaw would tighten up, knowing by the signal that she'd set her mind on something. "You're a cynic, Madeline."

"Yes, and you're a fool. How long have I been saying hire somebody? But no. Don't need a driver, do we?"

"Now you know damn well that I tried to hire someone."

Madeline rested her hand on one hip, jetting it out for effect. "Yeah. For slave wages. This isn't 1950."

Ida was incensed, cocking her head and drawing herself upright. "Arthur was perfectly happy with the arrangement. Never complained about his salary."

"Room and board plus two hundred a month was reasonable when he started. Fool stayed on."

"I don't want to hear anymore," Ida said, waving Madeline away with one hand.

"Shoulda taken a cab. But no, you had to take the

bus."

"Hush."

"Well, I'm calling Dr. Ross. Maybe he can stop by on his way home."

"You're calling no one. Don't need a doctor," she said, setting the tray aside and throwing off the covers. "Get my green dress out, and I want to wear my pearls."

"I don't think..."

"My green dress, I said."

~*~

The haunting dark brown eyes surrounded by yellow were so close to his own, too close, and the rank odor sent Junior's head tossing on his pillow. His face was damp with sweat and he made a gurgling noise as the fright overcame his sleep. He opened his eyes to see his own hand flailing in front of his face to ward off Cato's breath as he woke. When he realized it was a dream, he heaved a long sigh, wiping a shaky hand over his face.

The sunlight streaming through the slats of the Venetian blinds zigzagged across the thin blanket that was twisted around his legs. He hadn't slept much. He raised up on his elbows to see the clock. It was 8:00 am, and he was due at work by 9:30. He fought to unwind the blanket, seeing that it had left deep grooves in his dark legs and cut off the circulation to one foot. He eased out of the sagging sofa bed, favoring the bloodless, tingling left foot, and hobbled down the hallway in his boxer shorts. He pulled at the waistband of the boxers which had twisted in the night, bringing the fly back into position, and stopped for a moment to place his left hand in the small of his back and stretch. He heard a soft crack as he twisted his shoulders and felt relief in his spine from the sofa-bed-induced backache.

The bathroom tile was cold under his big feet as he leaned over the sink, lifting them one at a time. He looked into the mirror and thought he looked older.

Staring at his reflection, he began to plan his day: work for four hours, make the rounds of the pawn shops, hopefully raise enough money to keep Cato at bay. But could he do it, he asked himself? He wasn't sure he could.

He turned from the sink to run the water in the shower long enough to heat it up, striped off his boxers and stepped in, pulling the shower curtain closed behind him. He let the warm water stream over his face, squeezing his eyes closed and offering a small prayer that he could manage to see his way through this mess, remembering Ida's assurance that God didn't do these things and wishing he had her faith. He turned to let the showerhead focus on his back and rubbed the excess water from his eyes. He watched the trickles of sweat on the pale pink and gray tiles as they fought the heat to retain the cold they had accumulated all night. Then he watched them run down the walls and disappear into the water. He reached down for the bar of Ivory soap, seeing for the first time that Queen's shower cap was floating in the water beneath him. He fished it out and held it up to let it drain. He found that it was suddenly difficult to swallow and worked his upper lip against his lower teeth. He didn't want to cry.

~*~

The alarm clock ringing at 7:30 in the morning startled Maria Mendoza, bringing her forward in the chair she had fallen asleep in. She struggled to her feet, not noticing the paperback book as it slid silently from her lap onto the floor, and made her way to the side of the bed, punching the button atop the alarm to silence it. She saw the half-empty and now cold glass of milk she'd heated quietly at 2:00 and realized that it had worked, just not as fast as she'd hoped. She heard the boys roughhousing in their room as she walked to the closet. At eleven and twelve, they seemed to be forever pushing and pulling at each other, endless energy and constant conflict.

She opened the door to take out her robe and frowned, realizing once again there was no need to dress for work. From the back of the top shelf, the place where she usually hid her son's presents, the purse recaptured its claim on her conscience and she slumped slightly, resting against the door frame. It had robbed her of her sleep, that and the fear of having no income, and now it reasserted its firm grip on the coming day. "I had to," she whispered to the shelf, staring up as if waiting for an answer. She hadn't opened the purse, hadn't been able to muster the courage. She didn't want to know the old lady's name, see her face on a driver's license or find that she lived near the corner of her crime. She wanted her to live in some fine house surrounded with expensive furnishings, to have a box full of jewelry as impressive as the ring Maria had seen on her small white hand. She wanted it to contain only an expensive ladies' wallet with no identification of any kind, just money.

The high-pitched wail of little Julio's voice emitted a long seizure of the giggles, momentarily ending the purse's claim on her attention. When it shifted to one octave higher, she knew that Eduardo, the older of the two, was mercilessly tickling his little brother. She had to quiet them before the neighbors began to call. Glancing back up at the shelf, she crossed herself and closed the door.

CHAPTER FIFTEEN

"I said, two Diet Cokes," the young woman snapped, drumming the fingers of her right hand on the counter. "Not regular."

"Oh, right. Yeah. Sorry," Junior said as he took the two drinks back to the soda machine. He was having a hard time concentrating. Edgar watched Junior from his station, wondering what was bothering him. It irked him that Junior could be maddingly self-absorbed.

Junior returned with the correct drinks and handed them to the young woman. "Let's see, that's $12.28 altogether," he said, pushing the bag of hamburgers forward. She took out a $20 bill and handed it to Junior.

With a pinging sound, the cash register drawer shot open, and Junior lifted the till to hide the twenty below it. They had been busy today, and he paused at the sight of so much money, easily $700.00 worth. He bit his lip and picked up the stack of bills, fanning them with his thumb.

"Ah, excuse me," the young woman said, giving a impatient look, "is something wrong?"

Junior's head snapped up. "Oh," he said, "sorry,"

and he replaced the till and fished out her change, counting it out to her. She was the last of the current rush of customers and Junior was relieved to see her walk out.

Edgar walked over to lean on the counter next to him. "What's bugging you?" he asked.

"Nothing."

"I been watching. You're a million miles away, man."

Junior bent down and pulled the yellow pages from under the counter. "Do me a favor? Cover for me, okay. I have to make a phone call," Junior said, walking to the swinging door that lead to the back hall.

"Sure."

Junior leaned against the stark white wall, thumbing through the book, and stopped at pawn shops. He selected one close by and picked up the wall phone, punching in the numbers. He set the yellow pages down and pulled Ida's ring from his pocket, staring at it with a pained expression. The phone rang several times and was finally answered.

"Taylor's Pawn and Loan," a gruff voice said.

"I... " Junior hesitated, then abruptly hung up the phone. His stomach was in knots as he crammed the ring back into his pocket. He turned to see the manager's office door was closed and knocked lightly, opening it a crack.

"Excuse me, Mr. Burns."

William Burns looked up and motioned Junior into his little space. He was a heavyset black man constantly out of breath. The office was hot despite the roar of the window air-conditioning unit that ran the year around, and he fanned his face with a piece of paper. "What can I do for you? Not quitting on me, are you?" he said, looking concerned.

"No. Nothing like that."

"Okay. Shoot," he said, dropping the paper, leaning back on the squeaking desk chair and putting his hands behind his head. The circles of his sweat-soaked armpits stared at Junior.

"I need full time."

"Full time? What about school?"

Junior looked down. "I'm dropping out." He found the words embarrassing.

"Part time is all we have here. You know that."

"I thought... well, maybe you'd consider me for a night manager?"

"Already have two night managers. 'Sides, we both know you're not cut out for a career in fast food," Burns said, narrowing his eyes, wondering what had happened to make Junior want to give up the classes he talked about constantly. Whatever it was, he knew it had to be serious.

"I need more money. I really need to earn more."

Mr. Burns shifted forward in his chair, resting his forearms on the desk and clasping his hands together. "What's the problem, Junior?"

"My mother ran off with... with all our money," he said, feeling his face flush.

"She'll be back."

"Someday, maybe. Last time it was three years."

Mr. Burns stood up. "Sorry. Just don't have any full time." He reached into his pocket and pulled out a wad of bills. "Loan you a couple hundred, though. Tie you over, maybe?"

"No. Thanks, but no."

~*~

Ida stood in the bay window next to the Christmas tree, holding back the lace curtains, looking out. She frowned at the tall grass that nearly hid the sidewalk from view, wondering why the gardener had quit three weeks ago without saying anything. She didn't notice as Madeline entered the room, stopping to shake her head at what she saw as another disappointment for Ida.

"Why don't you come in the kitchen? Make you a nice cup of tea," Madeline said, knowing what Ida was thinking.

"Since when do I have to sit in the kitchen to get my tea?"

"Since you started staring out that window. Been in here all day. That boy just isn't coming."

"Is too."

Madeline looked over at the photo of Ida's son on the mantle and shook her head again. Always waiting for someone to come, she thought sadly. "Now, don't go taking offense. I know it's a disappointment. Kids just aren't the same these days, are they?"

Ida let the curtain drop and turned to face Madeline. "This one is different," she said, her eyes pleading to be right. "He'll come."

"Suit yourself, then," Madeline said, turning on her heel. "I'll get your tea."

CHAPTER SIXTEEN

The windows of *Grant's Pawn and Loan* were crowded with other people's pain; guitars, portable radios, laptop computers, rings, and strands of fake-looking pearls. A bicycle hung from the rafters over one of the windows with a Christmas sale sign stretched across it. Junior wondered if someone would receive the guitar for Christmas and how long it would be before it was back in this same window. This was his fourth pawn shop, the others refusing to deal with a nineteen year old sporting an obviously valuable piece of women's jewelry. The last one at least was kind enough to suggest this one and another closer to home he hadn't seen in the yellow pages.

Walking slowly to the door, he took a deep breath and entered the shop. A metallic buzzing sound alerted the pawnbroker, who stepped out of the back room quickly. Junior walked to the counter, looking down through the scratched glass top to see rows of rings, watches and other jewelry in little felt display boxes.

Mr. Grant approached, his chubby face devoid of any expression. He was a frumpy little man who had unruly hair and wore tortoise shell glasses with dirty bifocal lenses twice as thick as the countertop. He was as white as you could get short of being albino, and Junior wondered if he ever left the shop. "Help you?" he said.

"Yes. Yes, I've got something to pawn. Just temporarily, though. Not for long."

"I'm sure," said Mr. Grant, smiling for the first time, having heard that line a thousand times. "Let's see what you've got?"

Junior took the ring from his pocket, staring at it for a long moment, not wanting to hand it over. He looked up to see Mr. Grant's eyes struggling to focus on the ring at a distance. He was obviously interested. Junior handed it to him, feeling ashamed.

Mr. Grant made a little humming noise as he withdrew an eyepiece, bending close to inspect the stone. "Nice ring. Very nice ring." He returned the eyepiece to his pocket and looked inside the band. He looked up, pausing to focus on Junior's eyes as if he were debating his decision. Junior felt sure he was about to turn him down just like the others. "Could do nine hundred," he said.

"Nine hundred? Just nine hundred?" Junior was taken by surprise.

"That's it. Take or leave it."

"I thought it has to be worth thousands? Is it fake?"

"No. It's not a fake. It would probably cost eight to ten thousand new. But I don't buy new rings, do I?"

"It's not enough. I need twenty-two hundred dollars. Twenty-two hundred minimum," he said, thinking that, added to his grandmother's four hundred, he could repay Cato and still pay the rent.

"You have provenance?"

"Providence?" Junior said, mispronouncing the word, not knowing what it meant.

"Provenance," Mr. Grant repeated, stressing the *nance*. "Papers. Something to prove you own it. Its history."

"Well... uh... no. But I didn't steal it, if that's what you're worried about. Nobody's going to come looking for it."

"Without provenance, I am taking too great a chance. Nine hundred is my best offer."

Junior realized that no matter what he said, this man thought he was dealing in hot property. He reached over and took the ring back. He put it in his pocket and walked to the door. "What time do you close?" he said, looking back over his shoulder.

"Nine tonight."

"I'll think about it," Junior said as he walked out the door, hearing the buzzing sound again until the door closed behind him.

~*~

Junior stood in front of Mr. Thomas' door, wondering just how much he should tell him, how much he needed to know. He dreaded asking to borrow money from anyone, let alone his mother's only friend and the one neighbor that spoke to him, but the last pawnbroker had offered him even less than Mr. Grant had, thinking Junior needed it for drugs, no doubt. He realized that he was putting off what had to be done and knocked forcefully on the door, knowing the old man was hard of hearing.

He heard the shuffle of Mr. Thomas' feet and saw the light obscured in the little peephole. He mustered a meek smile as the door opened. "Well, Junior," he said, smiling broadly, revealing two missing teeth. The greasy smell of fish frying wafted into the hallway from behind him. "What can I do for you? Miss Eula's all right, isn't she?"

"Gramma's fine. I... I need to borrow twenty-two hundred dollars, Mr. Thomas," he blurted out nervously, surprising even himself. "I... ah... need it bad, or I wouldn't be asking." Without thinking, he dug Ida's ring out of his pocket. Mr. Thomas looked stunned, but before he could answer, Junior handed him Ida's ring. "I can give you this for collateral."

Mr. Thomas shook his head as he admired the diamond ring. "Twenty-two hundred dollars?" he said slowly and held the ring out, returning it to Junior. "I don't have that kinda money, son. Wish I did, but I only got $90 between me and the next check. You in some kinda trouble?"

"We just need it is all," Junior said, taking the ring back, his smile disappearing.

"It's that Mae, isn't it? She in some kinda trouble?"

"No," Junior said, knowing his grandmother wouldn't want him spreading gossip even if it were the truth. "Thanks anyway."

"Wish I had it. Give it to you in a minute if I had it," he said to Junior, who was already halfway down the hall.

Junior turned when he reached his door and said, "I know," and he went in, leaving Mr. Thomas to shake his head.

"Praise the Lord," Eula said, seeing Junior return. "Home safe."

"Home safe, Gramma. Cato didn't come by, did he?"

"No. What about the ring?"

"Still have it."

"Good," Eula said, looking relieved.

"It's not good. Could only get nine hundred for it."

"I'm glad. Wasn't our ring to sell."

"I wasn't selling it!" he snapped, overcome by the pressure of his grandmother's pious remark. "I tried to pawn it. I'd have gone back for it. I'm no thief."

"I know that, Junior," Eula said, realizing she had offended him.

"I didn't pawn it because I hoped I could borrow the money. But it's no use."

"I been praying over this," Eula said. "I think we

should call the police."

Junior began to pace, feeling the frustration of being caught between his naive grandmother and the facts of life. "You just don't understand, do you? We have to live here. We cross Cato and there'll be hell to pay."

"The police could keep him away."

"Not forever. For a day maybe, but it would only make Cato mad and then he'd really make our lives hell."

"Then what?"

"Give me the four hundred. I'm going back to the pawn shop. Maybe it'll be enough to keep Cato happy until I can figure out how to get the rest."

"No, don't. Let's pray over it tonight. Maybe Mae will come home."

"Time's almost up, Gramma. It can't wait 'til tomorrow."

"Under the mattress," Eula said, looking defeated.

Junior went to his grandmother's bedroom and returned, shoving the money into his pocket. He bent down and gave her a kiss on the forehead. He went to the front door and opened it. "Lock the door and don't open it for anyone," he warned her.

Eula watched the door close, staring at the knob for awhile before rising to lock it. She shuffled slowly back to her chair and opened her worn Bible to Matthew and began to read out loud.

~*~

Ida had barely touched her chicken and Madeline was almost through with her entire dinner. She was like a child, Madeline thought, hated to be disappointed. Still, Madeline wished she'd finish her dinner. "Eat up, now. We still have half a pie," she said, watching Ida's feint smile as her fork tried to hide some of the peas under the mashed potatoes.

The telephone rang and Ida sprang to life, sliding

away from the table. Madeline wondered if she just wanted an excuse to stop eating or if she was really expecting a phone call. "It's probably Junior," Ida said.

Madeline watched through the open French doors as Ida went to pick up the phone on the small table in the living room and called after her. "You gave him your phone number, too?"

"Of course I did," Ida said, picking up the receiver.

Madeline shook her head and ate the last four peas on her plate.

"Yes... yes, it is. No. No, thank you, we don't have carpeting," Ida said, slamming the receiver down.

Madeline watched Ida return from the corner of her eye, looking down when she neared, not wanting Ida to interpret her concern for an *I-told-you-so* look.

CHAPTER SEVENTEEN

It was thirteen blocks to Central Avenue through the turf of two warring gangs, so Junior made haste but carefully, not wanting to go either too fast or too slow. He knew the danger signs and listened carefully to the conversations within earshot. He understood enough Spanish to make out any hint of a threat from that faction of the ongoing conflict. Still, it was nerve-wracking, being so close to home but so far afield. Like being in a foreign country, he thought.

When he reached Central, he turned right and felt comfortable increasing his stride on a busy thoroughfare. It was nearly 8:45 and he still had two blocks to cover. In his haste, he hadn't noticed the big white Cadillac that had picked up his trail a good eight blocks ago, coasting at a safe distance and waiting for the right opportunity.

The neon sign that included the traditional three ball symbol of pawnbrokers had an eerie glow in the settling mist of what would shortly be a foggy night. He felt some relief as he turned into the alcove and reached for the doorknob. But something was wrong. It didn't want to turn in his hand. He rattled it, pushing and pulling, thinking which way did it open, in or out? It wouldn't budge.

Junior stepped back from the offending door and his heart sunk, seeing the cockeyed sign hanging in the side window. *Closed.* "No!" he yelled. "No, dammit!" and he returned to peer through the glass door. The clock over the far wall read 8:50, and he banged on the frame of the door.

"No!" he said again, softly.

In one last fit of frustration, he kicked the bottom panel of the door. From inside, an alarm bell sprang to life, ringing sharply, startling Junior and sending him running down the street.

Junior ran for three blocks, turning off of Central, mumbling to himself about his bad luck and the unfairness of his situation. He didn't notice the fog that swept about the streets, circling the cars and trash cans and slowly swallowing his peripheral vision. Nor did he realize that the big white Cadillac had done a U-turn as he ran from the pawn shop and was now inching up behind him.

After six blocks at full clip, his lungs began to ache from the ever-shortening breaths he was able to gulp down. He slowed first to a trot and then finally stopped to bend over, gasping to catch his breath. He felt a little queasy and swallowed hard.

Cato cruised to the curb alongside Junior and rolled down his window without Junior noticing him. "Looking for me, boy?" he said, spreading his lips to an oily grin.

Junior's head swiveled to the right, seeing Cato sideways from his bent position. He was speechless, still breathing heavily from the long run, unable to answer.

"Got my money?" Cato said as he pulled the door handle from inside the car and it began to open.

Junior straightened up quickly. "I need a little... more time, Cato," he said, panting his weak reply.

"Got no time, boy. Time's up."

Junior broke into a run when he saw Cato's feet touch the pavement. He tried his best to duplicate the speed that had carried him this far from the pawn shop, but there was little strength left in his legs and his lungs were now on fire. He heard the heavy footfalls behind him growing louder and he told himself he was not winded, he was not tired. But Cato caught up with Junior less than a block from where they'd started, grabbing him by the collar of his sweatshirt and slamming him to the ground on his back without letting go. The fog helped obscure the otherwise brightly lit street corner. There were no other signs of life on the street, no one to witness the chase or the fall, the fog having sent everyone indoors.

Junior rolled and twisted, trying to free Cato's grip on his shirt, but it was no use. When he stopped fighting, Cato lifted him with amazing ease by his left-handed grip on the shirt to a standing position. Junior shoved his hand into his pocket, withdrawing the four hundred in 20s and holding them out to Cato.

"What's this?" Cato said, frowning as if Junior had been holding out on him.

"Here... Four hundred... All we got," Junior said, still unable to catch his breath.

Without saying a word, Cato punched Junior in the stomach with his free hand, sending the 20's floating through the fog and scattering them along the curb. With the last of Junior's wind knocked from him, he doubled over in pain, trying in vain to suck in some much needed air, making a long, rasping noise in his throat.

"Don't hear too good. Do you, boy? Said two grand," Cato said, slowly, deliberately. He raised Junior closer to his level and slammed his right fist into Junior's cheekbone with so much force, spittle and blood sprayed from his mouth, spotting the pavement. Cato fought to hold Junior up from the sidewalk as he kneed

Junior in the groin with enough force to break his own grip on the sweatshirt and send Junior flying butt first, doubled in half into the side of the brick wall lining the sidewalk. Junior slid down the wall unconscious, his feet splayed in front of him and his head slumped onto his chest as if he were a drunk.

Cato took out a handkerchief, wiping the spit and blood from the knuckles of his right hand, then shaking the hand to relieve sting and stiffness that was already setting in. He walked to Junior's side and knocked him over with one foot. His head hit the pavement in a solid sounding thump. Cato bent down and began rummaging in the boy's pockets. He pulled out his wallet and tucked it into his shirt. From the left pocket of Junior's jeans, Cato extracted Ida's ring, standing to try and catch it in the fog-laden light. "Well. Well. Well. Now we're gettin' someplace," he said, shoving the ring into his pocket.

Cato leaned down to pull up his pants leg, withdrawing a buck knife that caught what little light there was, flashing it across Junior's bloody face. "Lesson time, boy," he said beginning to kneel down.

The brakes on the Arrowhead Water truck screamed as they always did in the damp weather as Jorge Juarez pulled to a stop under the streetlight. His headlights and two sodium fog lamps flooded the corner, catching the big blade of the knife raised above Cato's head. Jorge saw his face clearly as the black man stared into the light half-blinded. He also saw Junior's slumped figure on the sidewalk, the blood shimmering in the truck's lights. "Hey!" he yelled out the open window reflexively. "Hey, stop!" And he began to blow his horn, long blasts that shattered the quiet of the side street.

Cato jumped to his feet, tucking the knife from view, and ran back to his car. With a squeal of the Cadillac's tires echoing down the street, he reversed the remaining half-block and disappeared into the fog.

CHAPTER EIGHTEEN

The dinner plate jumped from Ida's hand when the phone rang, hitting the white tiles of the counter and shattering. Madeline gave her an unseen errant child look, but said nothing and continued to wash the dishes. "Oh, dear," Ida said, placing the dishtowel on top of the shards. She glanced at Madeline to see if she was angry, but she had already looked down, pretending not to have noticed. She went to answer the phone. Madeline rinsed her soapy hands and got the dustpan.

"Hello."

"Ida Hanson?" the deep-voiced male asked. Ida could hear the squawky voices and clicks of a police radio in the background, but didn't know that's what they were.

"Yes. I'm Mrs. Hanson."

"Detective Dawkins, LAPD, Mrs. Hanson. Sorry to bother you, but we have a young man here we're trying to identify."

"A young man?"

"Late teens. African-American. Medium height."

Ida caught her breath, hoping it wasn't Junior but guessing it must be. "Junior?"

"You know him, then?"

"Well, maybe."

"He had your name and address in his pocket."

Ida's heart began to pump faster. "It must be him. Is he all right?"

"Suffered a bad beating. He's unconscious. Robbery, looks like," Dawkins said in little bullets, each one causing Ida to flinch.

"God. How awful," Ida said, prompting Madeline to set the dustpan down and draw nearer.

"No ID," continued Dawkins. "Are you related?"

"No. I met him yesterday. He was supposed to come by today."

"You know his full name? Where he lives?"

"Junior? Junior?" Ida said, digging deep to remember his last name. The nickel finally dropped, "Thomas. Junior Thomas. I don't know where he lives. Somewhere around Florence and Normandie, but I don't know the address," Ida said, recalling yesterday's nightmare.

"There's a whole lotta Thomases in L.A."

"I'm not much help, am I?" Ida said, wanting to do more.

"We'll track it down. Sorry to bother you."

"Wait!" Ida said louder than she had intended to be. "Where are you taking him?"

"King General."

"I'll come right over," Ida said, seeing Madeline's eyes grow into an *are-you-crazy* glare.

Madeline watched Ida replace the receiver, avoiding direct eye contact with her. But Madeline would not be ignored. "Come right over where?"

"The hospital. Junior's been hurt."

"It's nearly ten o'clock," Madeline protested.

"Call me a cab."

"But you hardly know the boy."

"A cab," Ida said raising her voice. "I owe him that much."

"Well, you're not going alone," Madeline said, picking

up the phone and dialing. "Honestly. Steals your ring and you're going to the rescue."

"He didn't steal my ring!" Ida shouted.

~*~

The tops of the palm trees and the emergency room entrance were obscured as the cab nosed through the fog, sending its gray wisps swirling past the windows as it made its way up the long driveway. Ida didn't recognize any of it. When it finally came to a stop, she climbed out and handed the driver a twenty, not waiting for the change. Madeline struggled to catch up with her.

"Has to be gangs, you know?" Madeline continued the harangue she had started on the way to the hospital.

"He's not a gang member type," Ida said, growing tired of Madeline's negativity.

"Huh. As if you'd know. Now you be careful, you hear?" said Madeline as she rushed down the hallway behind Ida, who flapped one hand to dismiss her. Madeline sniffed the air, wrinkling her nose, thinking the place wasn't clean enough to be called a hospital.

Detective Dawkins closed the door to Junior's room behind him, seeing his graying mustache and unruly hair reflected in the little glass window. Need a haircut, he thought, a haircut and a cigarette. Since his wife walked out on him nearly a year ago, Dawkins had no one to remind him about his hair or anything else for that matter. He ran his tongue over his front teeth and sucked air between them, making a hissing sound, as he tried to clear the gaps of the residual pastrami from his hasty dinner. He wondered what his new partner of three weeks would say when she learned he hadn't called her. A rookie always expects a call, he thought. A pro would be glad not to have one. Besides, she was the one who'd gone home tired. Was it his fault he'd lingered? He didn't see it that way. He resented having another rookie. He didn't mind that it was a woman so much, some would but he didn't. It was the eagerness that bugged him.

He looked over to see two older women headed in his direction, one white, one black. He wondered what their relationship was, but he was sure the white one was Ida Hanson, her determinedly fast steps matching the mental picture he'd conjured from their phone conversation. She struck him as forceful, used to getting her way.

"Mrs. Hanson?"

"Yes," Ida said, coming to a stop abruptly, Madeline plowing into her. "You the detective that called me?"

"Dawkins, ma'am," he said, flashing a one-gold-tooth smile.

"This is Madeline," Ida said with a smirk, nodding her head toward her, "She's with me... I think?" she added for further castigation.

Dawkins smiled at the obvious friction between the two. "He's conscious now. No lasting damage. Looks worse than it is. Still, he's in a lotta pain."

"May I go in?" Ida asked.

"Yes. One question though?" Dawkins said, flipping through his notes. "He mumbled something about a ring. Wouldn't know what that's about, would you?"

"Ring? Why, yes. My ring."

"He had your ring?" Dawkins said, looking surprised.

"Yes. A diamond ring. I gave it to him for security. He didn't tell you about it?"

"Afraid he's not cooperating with us. Won't answer our questions."

It was Ida's turn to register surprise. "Not cooperating?" she said.

"Tried to sell it, I bet," Madeline said from behind Ida, unable to keep quiet.

Ida turned to give her the evil eye. "Shush!" she said and turned back to Dawkins. "He wouldn't sell my ring."

"Don't even know him," Madeline couldn't help but point out.

"Would you please be quiet?" Ida said through clenched teeth.

Dawkins was beginning to enjoy the two combatants.

"He's frightened of something. Maybe if you had a word with him?"

"Of course," Ida said, reaching for the door handle. "Wait here," she said to Madeline.

Pushing the door open quietly, she found the bed rumpled but empty. She entered and closed the door behind her. Stepping forward cautiously, she saw Junior struggling to untie the flimsy gown knotted behind his neck, one cheek of his buttocks peeking from the gape. "Ahem," she said, averting her eyes for a moment. "You shouldn't be out of bed."

"Damn," Junior said, giving up on the knot and turning to face Ida, wincing as he lowered his arms. "They told me you were coming. Thought I'd be gone by then."

"What's going on, Junior? What happened?" Ida said, approaching him. His face was badly bruised, his lips swollen and cracked. She wouldn't have recognized him. Her eyes dropped to see his crumpled, blood-spotted jeans on the floor beneath his feet.

"Nothing," he snapped. "I've gotta get home."

She could see the growing panic in his eyes and watched as his head swiveled slightly. "Tell me," she said.

"You don't want to get involved in this. It's danger..." he shook his head and squeezed his eyes shut. "Dangerous. Dammit." His torso began to weave and his head bobbed slightly.

Ida grabbed him by the arm, realizing he was about to pass out, and steered him to the side of the bed. He sat down without resisting, his mouth contorting as the pain rose from his swollen testicles. He felt a bit nauseous.

"I already am involved," she said softly. "Why won't you talk to the police?"

"I can't! I tell you. I can't."

"But why?"

"Stop pressuring me!" he yelled, lowering his head into his open hands.

"But the police can help if..."

"Dammit! Police'll just make it worse. If I finger Cato, he'll take it out on her."

"Her?" she asked.

"My gramma," he said, his voice growing pinched.

"Who's Cato? Did he do this?"

Ida suddenly realized that he was crying. It was something she hadn't been prepared for, and she struggled to maintain her composure. He was the young man who came to her rescue yesterday and yet here in the same hospital she saw that he was really just a boy. She sighed and took a seat next to him on the bed, her arm encircling his bent-over torso, feeling the convulsions as he whimpered.

"What is it, Junior?" she said softly. "Talk to me."

"I don't know what to do," he said, sniffling at first and finally sobbing openly. His right hand reached up to squeeze her left one where it rested on his shoulder.

"Talk," she said. "I want to help. It's my turn."

~*~

Ida pulled the door closed behind her, looking momentarily dazed, staring at the baseboard running along the wall across from her, not releasing the doorknob. Dawkins and Madeline rose from the two chairs they occupied opposite her, Madeline's chair legs screeching against the tiles as it moved backward under the pressure of her hands on the armrests and her weight as she rose. Ida looked up as if surprised to see them.

"You can go in now," she said, giving Dawkins a forced smile. "He'll tell you everything."

Dawkins nodded, noting the burden that the old woman had just assumed. He wondered about their story, about the ring, about so many things, but he knew this was not the time. He reached for the doorknob, turning to Ida, "Thanks." It was all he could think of to say.

"If you don't need us," Ida said, squaring her shoulders, "we'll be on our way?"

"I have your phone number," he said, turning the knob.

"Detective?" she caught him before opening the door, putting her hand on his arm.

"Yes?" he said, seeing her pale blue eyes search his.

"I promised him you'd take care of this," she said, dipping her head and looking up at him earnestly. "I don't want to be wrong about that."

He stared at her for a moment, absorbing the old woman's *promise me* look. "I'll see that you're not," he smiled. "Good night."

Ida watched to make sure the door was firmly closed, then turned quickly to Madeline. "Come on! No time to waste," she said pulling on Madeline's coat sleeve.

Madeline held back halfheartedly. "Oh-oh. Now what? Going home, aren't we?" she said as she found her feet moving forward against their will, her hand disappearing into the tugged on sleeve of her coat.

"One stop first," Ida said, increasing her speed and releasing her grip on the coat. She knew only too well that Madeline would follow.

"Where?"

"You'll see," was all Ida would say.

Outside the hospital, Ida frantically waved at a cab that had just pulled away. The driver saw her in his rear view mirror and his brake lights lit up. He backed up, Ida opening the door before he could stop. Ida shoved the reluctant Madeline into the back seat of the cab. "2120 Sheldon Avenue," she said to the cab driver, whose head turned abruptly at hearing the address. "Make it fast," she added.

"Sheldon? South Central Sheldon?" he said, dumbfounded.

"Yes! Go! Go!" Ida admonished him.

"South Central?" Madeline said, looking aghast.

~*~

It seemed to Madeline that all the windows of the buildings which sporadically appeared through the fog were barred and dirty. Graffiti changed languages, often unknown languages, as they passed from block to block. She didn't like this one bit and her scowl was only a hint as to how much.

"Bad neighborhood," Madeline mumbled.

"Oh stop," Ida said, not looking over at her.

"Dangerous," Madeline added.

"It's just a neighborhood you've read bad things about. No different from ours," Ida said, masking her own uneasiness.

"Well, you were attacked in this one, not in ours."

Ida had just about had it with her. "You've forgotten about our own sterling neighbors, haven't you? Remember the photographer three doors down? Got twenty years."

"One little incident," Madeline said.

"Child pornography isn't little. And Dr. Blevins? Killed his wife and two children just two blocks from us. Then there was the drug house."

"Things just happen," Madeline mumbled.

"Precisely," Ida said, looking away from Madeline and out her own window at a passing house. "Probably triple lock their doors just like we do."

The cab driver had kept an eye on the two warring women during the trip and was glad to finally reach their destination. "$6.30," he said, as he pulled to the curb.

"Wait here," Ida replied. "Leave the meter running."

The driver shook his head and frowned as Madeline watched. "I feel the same," she said to his image in the rear view mirror.

"Stay put," Ida said to Madeline. "I'll be just a moment."

Ida stepped from the cab, seeing the old man standing on the front steps. "Mr. Burke?"

"Yes, ma'am," he said, extending his hand to Ida. She took it and used it to pull herself up the stairs. Her feet were killing her. They disappeared beyond the scarred doors that banged shut behind them.

Madeline drummed her fingers on her knees and shook her head. "Lost her mind," she said under her breath. When the doors opened again, she saw Ida holding the arm of an old woman who seemed to have a difficult time walking down the steps. Mr. Burke followed them, carrying a weather-beaten suitcase. Madeline shook her head again. "Um-m-m."

"Miss Eula said Junior didn't make much sense on the phone," Mr. Burke was saying as he opened the front door of the cab to place the suitcase on the seat.

"No time to explain that now," Ida told him as she helped Eula climb into the back seat.

"Where are you taking her?" he asked.

"You don't need to know," Ida said, getting into the cab and slamming the door. "Anyone asks, tell them they're away for the holidays."

Mr. Burke leaned down to the open window. "Call me, Miss Eula, you hear?" he said, offering a big smile.

CHAPTER NINETEEN

Even though it was unmarked, the gray Crown Victoria, a color no one else would want, topped off with oversized black tires and an absence of chrome trim, was a dead giveaway. Everyone along the street in Fox Hills knew it was a police car as it pulled to the curb.

A dog-tired detective Dawkins climbed out, having had only four hours sleep. His new partner, Detective Denise Warren, exited from the other side looking fresh and ready to tackle the job even though she was mad as hell. She eyed Dawkins and frowned, but wasn't going to air her complaint just yet. She needed time to think. Two regular black-and-white units pulled in behind them, blocking the driveway.

Dawkins looked up and down the street, wondering what the neighbors in this up-market community thought of Cato. As he stepped up on the curb, he spit out the foul-tasting wad of nicotine-releasing gum, working his tongue against the roof of his mouth hoping to create some saliva to ease the dryness. Detective Warren, hot on his heels and fiddling with a notebook, managed to step on the wad of gum without noticing it.

Two of the officers fell in behind them as Dawkins

climbed the concrete steps and knocked on the aluminum screen door, not seeing the doorbell hidden behind the ficus tree. It was a pink house. Dawkins hated pink. He looked to his right, making sure the other two officers from the second patrol car had made their way up the driveway. He watched them disappear behind the house. The two behind him stood poised for action with their hands resting atop their holsters. Warren was scraping the sole of her shoe along the edge of the bottom step. He shook his head.

When Tina Nogales opened the inner door, she was barely visible through the screen. He could see her eyes, though, and they said nothing, making him wonder if she'd been expecting them. Dawkins flashed his badge, holding it briefly to the screen, then snapping it closed.

"Detective Dawkins," he said.

"So?" Tina said, shifting to one hip and leaning on the edge of the inner door.

"Like a word with Cato, ma'am."

"He's not here," she said without a trace of an accent.

"I have a warrant," Dawkins said, holding it up. Tina shrugged but said nothing. "Mind if we look around?"

"I told you Cato's not here."

Dawkins reached over and pulled the screen door open. The first thing he noticed was her black eye, and he wondered what it was she hadn't done or had for that matter. Tina saw him looking and turned her head.

"Wasting your time," she said, backing away from the door.

"Just the same, we'll have a look," he said stepping in, followed by the two officers and Warren, holding a pen and an open notebook. Stenographer, Dawkins thought. The place smelled of rancid cooking oil.

The two uniformed officers pulled their weapons, holding them high with both hands and fanning out. One went toward the kitchen, hesitating with his back to the door frame before entering. The other slunk along the wall of the hallway leading to the bedrooms. Warren reached into her jacket, stashing her notebook and unsnapping the strap of her holster, getting ready to follow the second officer. She took a step forward, but Dawkins grabbed her arm.

"Let the men do it," he said. He watched her head pivot back to glare at him. It wasn't what he'd meant. He knew she'd been one of them. It just wasn't her job, but he wasn't about to explain himself.

Cato watched from his mother's house across the street, two doors down. He smiled to himself and walked out the side door, getting into his Cadillac like a man of leisure and driving down the driveway. He stopped at the street for a moment, tempting fate. He enjoyed the thought of them snaking along the walls with their guns drawn as he watched right under their noses. He had given the boy more credit than to talk to the cops, but was pleased with himself for having taken the precaution of staying at his mother's house just in case.

Cato turned left, unable to resist driving past the patrol cars. The first thing he needed to do was find another set of wheels, and then he would have to deal with Junior. There was the truck driver, too, but that could wait.

~*~

Ida paid the cab driver, snapping her purse closed. She took Junior by the arm and walked with him up the sidewalk, jamming her other hand into her coat pocket against the chilly wind. She stopped suddenly, feeling the transfer slip still in her pocket, and pulled it out. She looked at it and then up at Junior. "Suppose it's no good now, huh?"

Junior smiled, "No. One day only."

They started walking again, Junior crouched slightly and taking short steps. The facial swelling had subsided somewhat, but his lower lip had gone blue-black and still protruded noticeably.

"Nice neighborhood," Junior said, surveying the area as he walked. He could still feel the pain in his groin, but the pills they'd given him had helped.

"House could use some work, huh?" Ida admitted with a frown.

"Why ride the bus?" Junior couldn't help asking.

"Why?"

"Yeah. Live in an expensive place like this and ride a bus. Doesn't add."

"Another Madeline," Ida said, stepping up her pace and ignoring the question.

They found Eula and Madeline sitting in the kitchen having coffee. Eula's eyes lit up momentarily at seeing Junior, but the look turned dark when she realized how battered he was. Madeline stared at him furrowing her brow. Ida thought the look was apprehensive, almost startled.

"You okay, baby?" Eula said, reaching to lightly touch his battered face as she stood up.

"Fine, Gramma. How about you?"

"Look at your face. Oh, Lord."

"It's okay. It'll heal," he said, taking her hand from his cheek and squeezing it.

"These ladies have been very good to me," she said, nodding at Madeline and Ida. "This is Madeline," she said, placing her hand on her shoulder. "Makes the best pancakes in Los Angeles."

Junior looked at Madeline, noticing she wasn't smiling. "Nice to meet you," he said.

"Your grandmother tells me you're going to be a doctor," Madeline said, breaking her silent stare but still unable to offer a smile.

"Goes to USC," Eula added.

"Gramma likes to think big," he said, knowing that he'd already made up his mind to drop out and find a full-time job.

"He's just modest. He's going to be a big doctor and take care of me."

"We need to talk about that, Gramma," he said, but she wasn't listening to him.

"Wait 'til you see the nice apartment they put us in," Eula said, beaming at her grandson.

"Don't get too used to it. They pick up Cato, and we'll be going home."

Ida took Junior by the arm. "Come. I'll show you around," walking him to the back door and going out.

As they crossed the driveway to Arthur's apartment, Junior noticed the overgrown flower beds and weed-choked grass, higher back here than in the front yard. Ida walked in the door ahead of him. "Hasn't been used for awhile. Not since Arthur died."

"Arthur?"

"Drove for me. Kept up the yard and the house, too."

"Oh," Junior said, looking around at the old but substantial furniture.

"Wouldn't know how to fix a lawn mower, would you?"

"Maybe. I'm fairly handy."

Ida smiled to herself, mumbling, "Hum."

"That a hint?" he said, seeing her thoughtful expression.

"Well, I wouldn't want to—"

Junior held up his hand, stopping her. "I'll do what I can to help while I'm here. It won't be for long, though, then I'm getting a full-time job," he said, his face sinking to a concerned look. "I appreciate your paying the hospital bills, but I plan on paying you back."

"We'll worry about that later."

"Pay you for taking us in, too."

"No need for that. Besides, I like your grandmother."

"Figured you would. You're a lot alike."

"Alike?"

"Yeah. Both think God protects you."

Ida caught the roll of his eyes as he said it and thought he was hard on God, but decided to let it pass.

"There's no telephone, I'm afraid," she said, changing the subject.

"Just like home."

"You can use my phone anytime. Could have one installed if you like?"

"Won't be here that long."

~*~

The heavy, sun-parched door of La Nuesta Senora De Los Angeles church slammed shut behind Maria. The stone floors and filtered light were cool compared to the warmth and glare of the sun she had just left. She stopped at the concrete pillar and dipped two fingers into the holy water, crossing herself and making her way down the aisle toward the little chapel on the left of the altar rail. Incense from the early Mass hovered above her, and her worn heels clip-clopped on the stones, reminding her that one of the hard rubber heel caps had fallen off, leaving the nail exposed.

When she saw the weeping statue of the Virgin, she averted her eyes. She was afraid to confront her and too tired and ashamed to go to confession. She had slept only fitfully since "the day of the purse," as she came to think of it, not the day she had lost her job, but "the day of the purse." But that was not why she had stopped by the church today. She had an appointment with a placement officer at the unemployment office, someone who was to help guide her search for another job, or so the brochure they had handed her said. She wanted to light a candle, wanted to ask the Virgin for help, not for her but for her two children. She knew she didn't deserve help, had no right to ask for it.

Maria watched the floor as she made her way down the short aisle to the rack of votive candle holders.

Digging in her purse, she withdrew two quarters and slipped them into the metal box, hearing the solid clunk they made as they hit bottom. It was empty. Odd, she thought, seeing that at least ten of the candles were shimmering, the red-beaded glass casting a glow over the black wrought iron holders. She fished out two more quarters and dropped them in too. With one of the white tapers, she lit three candles, one for each of her two boys and one in hopes of finding a job.

As she puffed out the lighted taper, she glanced up, unable to avoid the Virgin's presence above her. The Virgin appeared to be staring into the distance beyond Maria as if to ignore her. She quickly placed the taper back on the rack, turned and left the church.

CHAPTER TWENTY

Ida held the lace curtain back, watching Junior pushing the lawn mower back and forth across the front yard. It made a steady whine punctuated by the occasional ping of a rock being nicked by the blades. Sweat trickled down his face and his white T-shirt clung to his chest and back. Funny, she thought, I have to wear a winter coat and he's overheated. It was a big relief to see the sidewalk reappear after being obscured for several weeks.

Madeline cleared her throat as she entered the room, and Ida turned, offering her a big smile. "Suppose you want your tea in here?" Madeline said dryly.

"It's a nice sound, isn't it?" Ida said, ignoring her question.

"Sounds like a lawn mower to me."

"It would," Ida said, shaking her head. "It's the sound of a man around the house."

"They're not staying, you know," Madeline was quick to point out.

"You don't like him, do you?"

"Never said that. They're okay," Madeline said to Ida's back.

"Not they, him. I saw the way you looked at him when he arrived. You don't like him." She stared at Madeline, knowing she could read her face and count on it more than her reply.

Madeline stared back at her for a long moment. There was no way she could tell her how much he reminded her of Billy Lee. She'd hadn't spoken of him to Ida before and had no need to do so now. "I don't know him enough to not like him," she said, thinking it was perhaps a half truth. "Besides, it doesn't matter what I think."

"It matters to me what you think."

"Well, they're not staying. You heard them."

"We'll see," Ida said, turning back to the window.

~*~

Madeline looked both ways when she walked out the kitchen door. She wanted to make sure that neither Eula nor Ida were anywhere in sight. She walked into the garage and unlocked the driver's side door of Ida's old Cadillac and climbed in, deliberately slamming the door behind her.

The engine turned over several times before exploding into action. A stream of sooty exhaust spewed from the dual tailpipes and floated in the rear view mirror as Madeline watched for Junior. She had listened for the mower to stop, and she knew he'd be putting the lawn mower away soon. She wanted a chance to talk with him alone. She pushed both front window buttons and they descended with a whirring noise.

Maxwell, the neighbor's Great Dane, yapped wildly as Junior pushed the mower up the driveway toward the garage. He was used to Madeline and Ida but Junior was new. Madeline watched him hesitate at seeing the Cadillac's exhaust and then resume pushing the mower into the garage. She got out of the car, leaving it running.

"How old is this thing?" Junior asked, leaning into the passenger side window.

"Too old," Madeline said. "Hasn't been driven for over a year." She walked to the open garage door, leaning out. "Shut up, Maxwell!" she yelled and the dog stopped barking.

"Engine sounds pretty good," he said, looking up to see Madeline approaching.

"I start it twice a week," she said, noticing Junior's musky sweat smell.

"What about gas and oil?"

"Usually get the gardener to buy cans of gas and check the oil."

"Gardener," he said, perking up. "Why did I mow the lawn then?"

"Tried to raise his prices again last month. She had a kitten, so he never came back," she said, shaking her head.

"Is she low on money?"

"Ha! Low on reality is more like it," she said, returning to the driver's side and leaning in to switch off the engine. The exhaust had grown thick in the garage and she coughed and cleared her throat. "She's gonna want you to stay, you know?"

Junior frowned and shook his head.

"She's a good person," Madeline said, drawing nearer to Junior and looking him directly in the eye. "I don't want her getting hurt."

Junior didn't respond at first. He had known from the start that Madeline was a tough cookie, that she wasn't keen on their intrusion. He wondered how the two old women got along when no one was around. "Don't worry," he said finally. "We can't stay. Don't belong here."

"Don't belong?" Madeline found herself saying but wished she hadn't.

"We don't need charity. We can take care of

ourselves. When Cato's behind bars, we'll be out of here."

Madeline watched him walk out the door and wondered if she had been too harsh.

Junior leaned back, peering in around the garage door. "Thanks for being so nice to Grandma," he said.

Madeline felt a bit uneasy, but managed to say, "Sure."

~*~

Junior was lost in thought when he entered the guest house to wash up and change his sweaty T-shirt. He knew that it had been a warning and that Madeline was serious. He wondered why he had elicited so strong a reaction from her. It was obvious that she liked his grandmother and gone out of the way to make her feel welcome, but she didn't trust him. It was obvious.

As he passed his grandmother's door, he poked his head in to see if she was asleep. As usual, she sat in bed reading her Bible. "You okay in here?" he asked.

"Just fine," she said, closing the Bible. "What time is it anyway?"

Junior glanced at his watch, wiping the sweat from its crystal face. "Nearly two. Why? You got a date?"

"I'm gonna help Madeline stuff some peppers for dinner."

"No kidding," he said, surprised. She hadn't shown any interest in cooking for a long time. He did most of it himself. "You must be feeling pretty good then?"

"I like to help and Madeline is good company."

Junior walked in and stood by the window, looking out into what he soon realized was another yard beyond the garage and guest house. A stand of old fruit trees, some with split trunks, stretched for a good fifty feet back into the yard where a high slump stone wall separated it from another neighbor. The grass was even higher there than what he had just finished mowing.

Back to the mower, he thought.

"Madeline is not too keen on me, you know?"

"Whatever gave you that idea?"

"Just a feeling," he said, deciding not to go into her warning and the unsmiling face he saw each time he encountered her. Eula didn't respond but made a mental note to watch them together. She hoped he was wrong.

"Worried about Mae," she said, changing the subject. "What if she comes home and no one's there. What if Alvin is out playing poker when she comes?"

"She's gone, Gramma. You read the note. If we're lucky, it'll be years."

"She'll be back," Eula said, placing her hand on her Bible in a silent prayer. "Police wouldn't get after her over this, would they? I mean, she can't be held responsible for Cato, can she?"

"No. But I do."

"God is her only judge, Junior."

"Look. Let's not get into all that now," he said, realizing a sermon was about to follow. "Let's just hope they catch Cato soon, and we can go home."

"Amen."

Junior walked to the door ready to tackle the rest of the yard and get it behind him so he could shower.

"Probably need to be thinking about some kinda gift for Madeline and Ida, you know?" Eula said, stopping his exit.

"With what?"

"God will provide."

Junior shook his head, chuckling to himself, and left.

CHAPTER TWENTY-ONE

The plastic guard around her side view mirror scraped the concrete block wall as Warren pulled into her space four floors below ground, gritting her teeth. It was the third time this week she'd done it, lost in thought and paying little attention. She turned off the engine and leaned over to comb her short, brown hair and applied some lip gloss before climbing out of the car and snaking along the wall.

As she punched the elevator button, she tried on each of the opening lines she'd worked out last night. When she got the promotion, she knew it would be rough fitting in with the all-male detectives, but she was determined not to fail. It was just her luck she'd be assigned to Dawkins. He was the oldest of the lot, broodingly quiet and divorced to boot. No one had said anything bad about him, but he wasn't Mr. Popularity either.

Riding up in the elevator moments later, she found herself wondering what his wife had been like. It's not easy being married to a detective. It had to be even harder to live with a stoic like Dawkins. She suspected he held women in low regard. At least, that was how she imagined his treatment of her, and she knew she had run away. And in the three long weeks she'd worked with him, she felt like running away too.

When the doors opened, she stepped out, seeing her reflection in the windows opposite her, and stopped to cinch up the belt she'd loosened for the drive to work. As she continued down the corridor, she made a promise to pass on pizza and stick to salad at lunch for the entire month.

Dawkins was sitting behind his desk hunched forward staring into his computer screen when Warren walked into the office. At first, she thought he wasn't there and clinched her fists in frustration. She was loaded for bear. She'd had enough. Then she saw his left shoulder protruding from the side of the monitor and cleared her voice to get his attention. "Ahem."

Dawkins didn't look up from his game of Solitaire. He didn't much care who was there. "Yah," he mumbled.

"We need to talk."

"Oh, yah!"

"Yes. We need to clear the air here."

Dawkins grimaced to himself, hidden behind the screen, but let go of the mouse and pushed back in his chair, rolled it to the side and leaned forward, placing an elbow on the desk and resting his chin in his hand. He knew what her gripe was going to be. Rookie's lament, he thought. "All ears."

Warren moved forward, placing her hands on his desk and leaning forward for emphasis. "It's two weeks now, and you're not sharing. I don't know why. Maybe you don't like me, but it doesn't matter. I need to be in the loop."

There was that word, a woman's word, he thought. Sharing. She sounded like his ex-wife. "Sit. Talk," he said, gesturing with his free hand.

Warren pulled up a chair and took a seat. "Last week it was the drug raid. You knew about it before I left and didn't say anything." She watched his face for a reaction but got none. "The Chief was there. Was I there? No."

"Anything more," he said, knowing there was more to come.

"You could have called me when this assault was dropped in your lap. But no. You tell me the next morning on the way to the prep's house. On the way!" she repeated it, her voice rising.

Dawkins continued to stare at her. He wanted a cigarette. "I'm a man of few words."

"Few words! Hell, you barely speak. I feel like a leper."

"Listen. Calm down," he said, straightening up and pumping his open hand at her. "The bust I knew would happen but not when. You want me to say stick around? You want me to keep you here all hours?"

"The Chief was there, for cryin' out loud. What's he gonna think if he sees you and not me?"

"Trust me. He barely acknowledges seeing me."

"The Chief," she mumbled, ignoring his response.

"And the assault, it was 9 at night. I did you a favor."

Her hands shot up, palms spread, "No favors, please. Let me decide." She rose and began to pace the room. "We're supposed to be partners here. Supposed to share. I have to guess at everything."

For my sins, he thought, and he slumped forward, returning to his chin-in-hand pose. God he hated rookies.

~*~

Jorge Juarez pinched the gold crucifix through his cotton T-shirt, working it between his fingers as if trying to rub Jesus from his cross. Each question felt like an attack. He didn't like being alone with the two detectives, but his wife Rosa had refused to enter the police station, remaining in the car with the little ones. Her admonition to say nothing, however, was there somewhere under the cross.

Dawkins leaned back in his chair, holding the pencil with both hands that had so far been of little use, rolling it with his fingers. "You had to have seen it," Dawkins said, knowing Jorge was afraid and wondering if he should play friend or foe.

"It was very dark. It all happened so fast."

"Could it have been a red Cadillac?" Dawkins asked, purposely changing the color of Cato's car.

Detective Warren flashed her eyes at Dawkins and almost corrected his error before realizing what he was up to. She caught her lips mid-gape about to say "white". Another case of his not clueing her in, leaving her in the cold. It was her first official interrogation as a detective and her left foot wiggled nervously in the air suspended from her crossed leg. Until now she'd only played tag along, and he'd promised to let her join in. As she turned back to watch Jorge, she got a whiff of her perfume, making a mental note to suspend its use for awhile. Maybe that's what he doesn't like, she thought.

"Maybe, I don't know," Jorge said, his lip twitching.

"But it was big, right?" Warren added, wanting to say something, anything for the record. She jotted a quick entry in her notebook as if every word could be a future clue. When she looked up, Dawkins forced a smiled for her sake, thinking her eager but pointless scratching was the first thing that had to go. She smiled back, wondering what he was thinking, why he'd smiled.

"Big. Yes," Jorge said, eyeing her from the side, wishing she weren't in the room.

Dawkins leaned forward, changing his expression to a frown, opening a file and taking out a stack of mug shots. "Take a look at these," he said, handing them across the messy desk to Jorge.

Jorge pretended to study the first few black faces. The fourth photo was Cato's and he tried not to glance up but did so very briefly, looking back and rifling through the rest.

"No familiar faces?" Dawkins said, knowing he had recognized number four.

"No," Jorge said, avoiding Dawkins' eyes and handing the stack back to him.

"You're sure about that?"

"Yes."

Dawkins shrugged and shook his head. "I guess that's it."

"I can go?" Jorge said, surprised.

"Yes," Dawkins said, seeing the puzzled look on both Jorge and Warren's faces.

Jorge stood and walked to the door quickly, rolling his eyes to the ceiling in a silent thank you to the Virgin Mary.

"Mr. Juarez," Jorge heard Dawkins say from behind him. He pinched his eyes shut, hoping he hadn't changed his mind. Jorge turned slowly. "Yes?"

Dawkins shook his head again, thinking better of asking if he'd been contacted by Cato or one of his friends. "Nothing."

Jorge left before Dawkins could change his mind.

The moment the door closed, Warren leaned forward. "He recognized Cato," she said as if it were a news flash.

"Yeah," Dawkins said, absentmindedly reaching for a piece of nicotine gum, "and he saw the car, too." He stared at the foil wrapper and tossed it back into the drawer. He wasn't sure which was worse, quitting smoking or weaning himself off this stuff.

"Cato got to him. Ten to one," Warren said. Dawkins raised his eyebrows and shrugged slightly. Warren resented his many nonverbal communications. "Is that a yes or a no?" she asked.

"Maybe," he said.

The phone buzzed. Dawkins sneered at it. He hated the idea of a buzzing telephone. What was wrong with ringing? He stabbed the line button with one finger and picked up the receiver. "Dawkins," he said, staring down at his well-chewed fingernails. "Whadaya mean you can't find him? You found his car?" He grew annoyed, listening to the lame excuse. "Okay. Make the rounds. I want him, and I want him quick." Dawkins stood up, stretching his neck as he listened and turned to look at the cheap, sun-faded reproduction of a California landscape. He never had been able to read the artist's signature. "What about the ring?"

He turned around and Warren saw his eyes register interest. "You don't say? Same day, huh? Well. Well. Well. Thanks," he said and abruptly hung up.

Expecting a big break in the case, Warren waited for an announcement. She could see his mind working, but he said nothing. Would it always be this way? Frustrated, she asked, "So?"

"Found his car. No sign of Cato," he said absentmindedly, not looking at her.

"The ring?"

"Junior, the little angel, tried to pawn it."

"There's a twist," she said, jotting another note in her little book.

"We'd better have another talk with him."

~*~

The worn white, vinyl top and dented left front fender made the car less than ideal for someone not wanting to be recognized, but the price was right. Free. Cato called it the LAX Auto Mart, drive into the airport parking, dump what you're driving, wait for someone with bags to park and you got yourself a car. With luck, the owner wouldn't be back for a few days at least, which you could judge by the amount of baggage being lugged. He cruised to the curb, scraping the whitewall tires against it, not yet being used to its size. The Chrysler looked so much smaller than his Cadillac.

He checked the side and rear view mirrors before

getting out and crossing the street, entering the apartment building without being seen. He took the small wire device from his pocket and inserted it in the first lock, tweaking it gently until he heard the click. He ran his Bank of Los Angeles ATM card down the gap in the door, releasing the lower lock, and entered Junior's apartment. Moving silently down the hall, he checked each room but no one was home. He returned to the telephone in the hall to check the message pad, but it was blank. He held it up to the light sideways, but no grooves were evident. Whatever the last note taken, the writer hadn't applied sufficient pressure to leave a ghost.

He entered the living room, looking for any telltale signs. Nothing leapt out at him. He was pretty sure Junior would be in one of the hospitals, but he wanted to find out what Queen's mother knew, where the police had moved her for safety. No luck, though.

He headed for the door but stopped as he reached for the handle and turned around. Walking back to the phone, he picked up the receiver and hit *69. After two rings it was answered, "King General. How may I direct your call?" the voice said. Cato smiled.

Leaving the apartment, he pulled the door closed as quietly as he could, hearing the lower bolt click into place. He didn't bother to lock the upper one.

As he turned to leave, an old man walked out of the adjoining apartment. Cato smiled and pretended to be knocking on Eula's door.

"Nobody home," Mr. Burke said, returning Cato's smile.

"When will they be home?"

"Away for the holidays," Mr. Burke said, wondering who Cato was and trying to etch a picture of him in his mind for future recall.

Cato eyed the old man, knowing he was lying to him. He wanted to beat the truth out of him but knew better.

"Can I tell them who came by?" Mr. Burke said, hoping to get his name.

"Nah," Cato said, walking toward the door. "I'll give them a ring after when they're back."

CHAPTER TWENTY-TWO

Ida had expected to find the two detectives sitting when she entered the living room. But like two cats, Dawkins was looking at the photos on the mantle and Warren was fingering the various ornaments on the Christmas tree. She watched as Warren rotated a silver glass figurine her husband had bought for her in the orient and wondered if all detectives were naturally curious.

"Hello, Detective Dawkins," Ida said, watching him replace her wedding picture, careful to see that the easel held it upright. "You wanted to see us?" Ida noticed that the woman only looked over her shoulder for a moment.

Dawkins approached her, smiling. "Actually, we wanted to have another word with Junior. No need to bother you, Mrs. Hanson."

"Well, I naturally assumed I should attend, too. You don't object?"

"No," Dawkins said, realizing she came with the package.

"Hotai," Ida said, turning to look at Warren, thinking she was rude for not acknowledging her entrance and not introducing herself. Warren finally turned, offering a broad but quizzical smile. "Hotai," Ida repeated, "the God of Happiness or balance and abundance. A Buddha, really. I've never seen another one in glass."

"It's quite fascinating," Warren said, settling back into place carefully and coming to join them. She reached out her hand to Ida. "I'm Detective Warren," she said. "You have a lovely tree. So many neat ornaments."

"Thank you," Ida said as she shook her hand, noticing that Warren's nails were painted an unexpected pink. "That one is from Singapore. My husband bought it for me while we were on our honeymoon."

"What a thoughtful gift for a new bride."

"Why, yes. Yes it was."

"Probably worth a fortune. There's quite a market for old stuff like that. Looks like you have a lot of old stuff," Warren said.

"Old," Ida repeated, disliking the expression and thereby the expresser. "Yes, I guess you'd think so."

"Is Junior here?" Dawkins interrupted the two women, feeling the chemistry growing tense. Funny how some women rub each other the wrong way, he thought.

"Yes, Madeline has gone to get him. Would you care for some tea," Ida said, looking only to Dawkins.

"No, thank you."

Ida took a seat on the sofa, motioning for Dawkins to join her and ignoring Warren. Dawkins sat down and Warren chose a chair facing them.

"Have you caught him yet?"

"No. It's just a matter of time, though," Dawkins said.

"Then what brings you here?"

"Couple of things," Dawkins said, interrupted by Junior entering.

"Got him?" Junior said, his voice excited.

"No, not yet," Dawkins said, watching Junior's expression sag.

"I've got to get back to my job. I could lose it," Junior

said, inching closer, his eyes never leaving Dawkins.

"Not yet. Not now."

"But you said it would be a matter of hours?"

"I know."

"I need the money. We have to pay the rent," Junior continued his protest.

"I think you'd better have a seat," Dawkins said, pointing to the chair next to Warren.

"Something's wrong?" Ida asked.

"It seems Cato has quite a record," Dawkins said.

"So," Junior said.

"Have you heard of the Three Strikes law?"

"Sure."

"If he's convicted again, he could get life. Especially given that assault with a deadly weapon is a felony."

"I don't understand?" said Ida. "Why should that matter to us?"

Dawkins turned his attention to Ida. "The truck driver has had a sudden lapse of memory. That means Junior's the only one who can identify Cato."

"And Cato will no doubt have an alibi," Warren added.

Junior's eyes darted back and forth about the room. He stood and walked to the window, staring out. "He'll come after me, won't he? Try to kill me?"

"Good heavens," Ida said, catching her breath.

"He may try," Dawkins said, trying to keep his voice even, placing his hand on Ida's arm. "The driver did tell us at the scene that he saw a knife in his hand."

"He may also have fled," Warren said, seeing Ida's panic.

Dawkins' eyes were trained on the back of Junior. "Do you want to tell us about the ring, Junior?"

"The ring?" he said without looking back.

"Yes, the ring," Dawkins repeated.

Junior turned his head, looking at Ida from the corner of his eye. "Cato took it."

"Is that right?" Dawkins continued.

"Must have," Junior said.

"Owner of a pawn shop near where you were assaulted says a young man came in that same afternoon, much earlier though. Says he tried to pawn a ring. A diamond ring," Dawkins said, pausing. "Was that you?"

Junior walked back to the chair, working his lips one against the other as if they were chapped. "I... I did, yes." Ida looked up at him. Her expression was one of shock. "I needed the money," he said.

Realizing she was making it difficult for Junior, she softened her look. "Yes. Yes, of course, you did."

"And you didn't hock it somewhere else?" Dawkins said.

Junior looked insulted. "No. I went back, but he was closed. That's why I was near there."

"You're sure about that?" Dawkins said.

"Honest. Cato took it."

"Why is the ring so important, anyway?" Ida said.

"If we arrest Cato, we'll need it to shore up Junior's testimony."

"You don't believe me, do you?" Junior said, leveling his eyes on Dawkins.

"We don't work on beliefs. We work on facts, Junior," Dawkins said, rising from the sofa.

"You think I beat myself up?"

"No. The truck driver saw that," Dawkins said, and then he sprang his surprise question. "You weren't trying to work a deal with Cato for the ring?"

"I told you, I tried to give him the four hundred I had. He hit me. I don't remember anything else. Okay?"

"You're absolutely sure you didn't hock the ring anywhere else?" Warren asked.

Junior turned to look Ida in the eyes. "I swear," he said, his hand rising for the oath.

Ida shook her head. "All this over two thousand

dollars."

Dawkins looked down at her. "Prostitution. Drugs. They both depend on fear to keep people in line. It could have been a hundred," he said.

Warren looked over her notes and placed one hand on her hip in what Ida found a very unfeminine pose. "Is there anything else you haven't told us?"

"No. Nothing," Junior said, half raising his hand for an oath again.

"Positive?" Dawkins said.

"Yes," Junior said, adding, "what now?"

"Stay low," Dawkins said, moving toward the entry hall. "Above all, stay away from South Central."

Ida lead Warren and Dawkins to the front door, catching from the corner of her eye the kitchen door being eased shut to prevent over-swing. She smiled to herself and opened the front door.

When both detectives had safely passed her, she stepped onto the front porch, closing the door behind them. "You will provide protection?" she asked, looking earnestly into Dawkins' eyes.

Dawkins looked down at the car keys in his hand. "Best we can do is occasional drive-bys," he said, glancing up at Ida and looking off toward the street.

"You can't put someone on duty here?"

"Just don't have the manpower."

Warren saw the concern in Ida's eyes. "Try not to worry. L.A.'s a big city, and Cato doesn't know Junior is here."

"Yes, of course," Ida said, taking on a frustrated look.

"We'll get him," Dawkins added, walking down the steps. Warren stared at Ida, wondering if something else needed to be offered but not knowing what it would be.

Ida went back into the house without saying any more. She found Junior waiting by the open French doors to the living room.

"I... " he began, faltering, unable to find the right

words to explain his failed attempt to pawn her ring. He wanted her to know that under any other circumstances he would never have thought of doing such a thing.

"You don't have to say anything," Ida said, realizing he was struggling. She understood his predicament even though it didn't lessen her disappointment.

"But."

"Not now," she said, lifting one hand to fend off further discussion. "I'm going to lay down for a few minutes."

It was a reflex action, one that he regretted even as the words escaped. "Lie down."

Ida's face reddened and a nervous twitch took her upper lip. "One thing you need to learn, Junior," she said as evenly as the out-of-control lip would allow. Junior gritted his teeth, realizing his offense. "Education is a tool and not a weapon," she said, walking to the stairs and climbing them slowly, not looking back.

~*~

Dawkins started the engine and picked up a pack of regular chewing gum from the dash, offering a stick to Warren.

"You believe him?" Warren asked, taking a piece.

He unwrapped his stick of gum, crumpling the paper and tossing it into the open ashtray which was already overflowing with similar papers. "Time will tell," he said, looking over at her. He hesitated for a moment, watching the side of her young face as she mulled over her own question in her mind. He rolled the flat stick of gum into a coil, releasing its minty scent, improving the stale air in the car. "Word to the wise?" he said, interrupting her thoughts.

Warren turned to look at him. "Sure. What?"

"Never tell an old person what they have is old," he said, shoving the stick of gum into his mouth and putting the car into gear. "Like it, period. Or call it an antique... but don't call it old."

He finally speaks without being asked a question, Warren thought, and what do I get? A lecture on manners.

Dawkins looked into the side view mirror and pulled away from the curb, enjoying for a change the bursts of spearmint instead of nicotine as he chewed. But he still wanted a cigarette.

~*~

Madeline clanged a cast iron skillet into position on the stove, thinking it was best to keep busy. She was stunned and frightened by what she'd overheard Dawkins saying and wondered how much of this Eula would be told. She opened the refrigerator door and stared into its shiny surfaces. A part of her wanted to gloat over her now-correct warnings to Ida. The danger was real. Bad things could happen. Deep inside, though, she knew that Junior and Eula were not the cause. They weren't the bad ones, but they'd brought it with them, and Ida needed to go even slower.

Madeline's head did a little shake, coming back to earth, realizing she'd forgotten what it was she wanted from the refrigerator. Cheese, she remembered. Cheese and butter. She fished them out and closed the door.

As she spread the butter and placed the slices of yellow cheese on the bread, she debated telling Eula how real the danger was. She assumed that Junior would not share the conversation, knowing she'd be frightened even more. Placing the sandwiches, buttered face down, into the hot skillet, she asked herself if she believed Junior's version of the pawn shop story, but more importantly, would Ida. She would, she thought. But Madeline wasn't sure.

A thick smoky smell of the burning butter gathered her attention and she quickly turned the two sandwiches over. They were burned only slightly.

She made her way to the swinging door, opening it and calling to Ida. "Lunch is ready!" She took out two plates and lifted the edges of one sandwich to see that it was almost ready. I can't tell Eula, she decided. It's not my place.

CHAPTER TWENTY-THREE

"You can drive, can't you?" Ida said as she pulled open one side of the garage door.

"Well, yeah. Sure," Junior said, opening the other side and looking for something to stop it from swinging closed. He kicked a good-sized rock from the weed-choked border into place. "Wait," he added, remembering one vital catch. "No license. Cato took my wallet."

"Formalities," she said as she entered the garage and walked to the passenger side door of the Cadillac, smelling the still-damp grass clippings that clung to the underside of the mower. "Need to hurry," she said, watching him standing by the open doors. "By three o'clock the place will be packed."

Junior watched Ida as she stood by the car door tapping her right foot on the concrete floor. "Oh, the door," he said, hurrying to open it for Ida. She didn't even smile. She hadn't smiled once yet, and he could still feel the tension from their earlier confrontation. "This could be dangerous, you know?" he said as Ida slid in.

"Nonsense. It's been perfectly maintained."

"Not the car. I mean Cato."

"We're not going to South Central. Going three blocks to the grocery store," Ida said, opening her purse and digging out two $100 bills. She handed them to Junior. "Here."

"What's this?" he said, looking at the bills and frowning.

"For mowing the lawn."

"Two hundred for mowing a lawn?"

"Once a week for a month," she said, snapping the purse shut and reaching for the open door.

"I can't take this," he said, refusing to back away, blocking her from closing the door. "We won't be here for a month anyway."

"How do you expect to buy groceries for your grandmother? Got a credit card?"

"No," he said.

"Just don't buy a turkey. Madeline always has turkey on Christmas day. Donald's favorite, and you're invited," she said, slamming the door and looking straight ahead.

"No, we couldn't," he said to the closed window, but Ida could still hear. "He'll want to spend the time with you. I mean. You haven't seen him for awhile, have you?"

She had a puzzled look when she turned to face him. "Seen him?" he heard her muffled voice say, and he watched her punch the power window button to no avail.

"He may not make it. Besides, Madeline is counting on you. Making more than enough."

Junior stuffed the money in his pocket as he walked around the car, thinking he should start a list of the money he owed Ida. He wasn't letting her pay him for mowing the lawn. He climbed in and started the Cadillac, seeing Ida facing straight ahead like a woman used to being driven.

Maxwell barked and raced along the fence as Junior

leaned out of the window, backing down the driveway, the exhaust making him blink.

~*~

When Edgar looked up from his stool, his shoulders jumped slightly, surprised by the large man staring at him. "Oh. Help you?" he said, mustering a smile.

Cato studied Edgar for a moment. He knew Junior had been released from the hospital yesterday. He wasn't home, and it didn't look like he was here either. Someone knew where he was. He rolled the toothpick to the other side of his mouth with his tongue before reaching up to withdraw it. His eyes never left Edgar nor did he smile back. "Junior working?"

"Junior?"

"Junior Thomas. Your friend, I hear," Cato said, raising his eyes to the kitchen door.

"Not exactly a friend," Edgar lied, fearing Cato might stake out his house watching for Junior.

"Whatever. He here?"

"No. Hasn't been in for a few days," Edgar said, reaching for the damp rag and nervously wiping the counter.

"Where is he?"

"Nobody tells me nothing," Edgar said, avoiding eye contact.

Cato continued to stare at Edgar, who glanced up at him occasionally. He reached into his pocket and pulled out $50 and waved it slowly under Edgar's nose. "Sure about that?"

Edgar stopped wiping the counter and looked at the bill, feeling just a little torn. "Honest," he said.

Cato's eyes drilled Edgar, waiting to see any sign of a change of mind. With no response, he stuffed the money back into his pocket and walked out.

Edgar started wiping the counter again, glancing up from time to time, watching Cato cross the parking lot and then the street. He walked to the window, straining his eyes to see as Cato drove away. He pulled the detective's card from his wallet, picked up the greasy phone receiver and dialed.

~*~

Dawkins punched the button on the first buzz. He was glad for any interruption, even the infernal buzz, tired of having Warren sit on the other side of the desk like a retriever waiting for him to toss the ball or "share" something.

"Dawkins," he said. Warren watched him straighten up in his chair at the news he was hearing and flipped open her pad, taking a pencil from the cup on his desk.

"When was that?... Okay... Model?" Dawkins said, scratching notes illegibly. Warren strained to read them upside down. "No. You did right. If he comes back again, let us know."

Dawkins replaced the receiver without looking up at his eager assistant and said nothing. It was starting to be a game with him. He felt a bit guilty not offering her anything, but he took a perverse joy in seeing how long it took her to ask.

"We got a lead?" she asked, thinking he was a jerk and the talk had gained her nothing. Hates women.

"Cato's still in town," he said, finally looking up. "Get an APB out for a gray late model Chrysler. Dented left front fender. Shabby vinyl top."

Warren was writing fast. "California plates?"

"Couldn't see 'em."

"Who couldn't see them?" she said, staring deadpan.

"The caller."

Warren tapped the end of the pencil on her notebook. It was now deadpan for deadpan—OK Corral, police style.

Dawkins blinked first. "Junior's friend at the burger joint."

Warren frowned and tapped again, this time louder and longer.

"All right. So I didn't tell you I spoke to him," Dawkins said, waiting for her response. When she said nothing, "I forgot. That's all. Just forgot," he raised his right hand.

Warren looked down at her notebook. "Name."

"Edgar-something. You want the address?"

"No, thanks," she growled, dismissing further discussion.

"Now will you get the word out?"

"Not much to go on," she said, standing to leave.

"It's a start," Dawkins said, thinking he was glad something had taken Warren out of his face.

~*~

Ida could only carry one of the six bags of groceries, and at that she trailed behind Junior with his two as he mounted the steps of the back porch. "Wait," she said, stopping suddenly to cock her head. Junior turned mid-step, seeing Ida's face take on an impish smile as she listened to the two women in the kitchen chatter away. "Sounds like a couple of schoolgirls."

Junior smiled, surprised to hear his grandmother talking and laughing. Perhaps Madeline wasn't so bad after all, he thought.

"Having a tea party?" Ida said as she entered the kitchen.

Madeline sprang to her feet and took the heavy bag from Ida's arms. "Just a chat," she said, looking away from the smile Junior offered her as he followed Ida in the door.

"Any more in the car?" Eula asked, getting up from the table.

The cans in one crumpled bag clunked as Junior set it down on the tile counter. The bag in his other hand he gripped from the rolled down top began to rip, and he did a quick knee-bend, resting it on the floor before the contents could scatter.

"Yeah, four more," he said. "But I'll get 'em."

Eula was already at the door. "I can help," she said, looking at her grandson.

"Not with your arthritis."

"Feel like a little exercise," she said, going out the door before further protest.

Junior spread his open hands, giving Madeline and Ida a surprised look. He followed her out, leaving them to put away the groceries.

"Looks like you bought out the store," Madeline said, surprised at the payload, used to one or two bags.

"Saved cab fare," Ida said, and Madeline laughed.

"You like Eula, don't you?"

"She's all right."

"Just all right?"

Madeline held a can of tomatoes in her right hand and turned to look at Ida as she lifted it into place in the cupboard. "What are you getting at?"

"Oh, nothing."

Junior and Eula came back in, setting the remaining bags on the kitchen table.

Ida continued to put things away, not wanting to make a big deal of what she was about to say. "Been thinking. It might be better if you two moved into the house." She watched Madeline's surprised look from the corner of her eye, knowing she wouldn't have gone along with her and making it difficult for her to object now.

"No. We're just fine where we are," Eula said as she began to take items from the bags and hand them to Madeline.

"Cato doesn't know we're here if that's what you're thinking," Junior said.

"Are you sure of that?" Ida asked, wishing she hadn't.

A large red apple bounced on the floor and rolled to

Ida's feet. She looked up to see the pensive expression on Madeline's face, the empty apple bag suspended from her hand and the other apples scattered along the tile counter.

CHAPTER TWENTY-FOUR

The brim of her gardening hat flip-flopped in the wind, obscuring, then revealing the rose hip she was trying to get at with the clippers. Reaching up, she pushed the hat back on her head by the crown and snipped the bright orange hip, sending it sailing to the side. Ida had forgotten how nice it was to putter in the garden. For two days she had ignored the bright sunlight that had greeted her each morning, demanding outdoor activity. And even after all the years she'd lived in California, she still found it odd pruning back the roses in December. But today she decided to attack the borders of the neglected house and that meant pruning the roses.

Moving down the line of the leaf-strewn and weedy border in advance of Junior, she looked back to watch him churn the earth with the rusty trowel. She would buy a new one next week, she thought, some rose food, too.

"Sure know how to pull weeds for someone living in an apartment?" she said, continuing her so-far-unsuccessful attempt to find a mutually agreeable topic and bridge yesterday's gap. She regretted snapping at him and then dwelling on it in her mind for the rest of the day.

"Worked for a gardener one summer. Dirty work."

"Rewarding, though. Watching a garden grow, keeping it neat."

"Still dirty," he said, busily digging, pulling and tossing the weeds and leaves behind him as he moved along. "I don't plan to be anyone's yard slave."

Another touchy subject, she thought, frowning to herself and shaking the thick stem of a rose, sending the dead leaves floating to the ground. "Ouch!" she said, pulling off her right glove and sucking on her index finger. "Thorns!"

Junior looked up. "It's a rose bush," he said dryly and turned back to his weeding.

Ida frowned. Faking a puncture wound hadn't done the trick. She started clipping again, adding nonchalantly,

"Donald used to help me with the roses, too."

"Never let the gardener do it?"

"Oh, no. No. Never."

"Why Donald? Why not Don or Donny?"

Ida paused for a moment. "Don or Donny... that's a good question. I really don't know."

"I think of Donald Duck every time you say his name."

"Really? I wonder if he ever thought that?" Ida said, stopping to reflect on it for a moment.

"Maybe I'll ask him?" Junior said, scooting down along the border on his knees.

"Ask him?" Ida said before realizing Junior was expecting him for dinner on Christmas day. "Yes. Well, perhaps it's better left a mystery."

The conversation at least started to melt the near silence that had existed between them since Dawkins' confrontation with Junior. So she decided to move it in the direction she'd had in mind all along. "What's going to happen when your mother comes back?"

Junior gave a grumpy chuckle, "Isn't likely. Gone for years at a time."

"But how will you survive?"

"Gramma and I will be fine. If anything, it'll be easier."

"But you'll have to pay the rent by yourselves," she said, assuming Queen had contributed to their expenses.

"That's why it'll be easier. She won't be borrowing anything from Gramma."

"How much is the rent?" Ida asked, finally getting to the questions she really wanted to ask.

The scraping of the trowel stopped as Junior turned to look at her. Pretending not to notice he was watching, she busily snipped away at the poor rose bush, already over pruned.

"Our rent?" he said, wrinkling his brow, wondering where this was headed.

"Yes. How much do you pay?"

"Six hundred. Why?"

"Oh, I was just thinking."

"Thinking what?"

"Well, that if you stayed here, rent free, of course, you could go to school full time."

"We're going home when this is over," he said, stabbing the trowel into the ground with great force. "We don't need charity. We can take care of ourselves."

Ida moved down the line to the next rose, ignoring the violent response to what she felt was a casual offer, something to think about. "It's just nice to have other people around and all," she said, shaking the next rose. "I was just trying to..."

Junior was on his feet before she could finish. "Stop trying!" he said in a loud voice, shaking his head, clamping his teeth shut and hearing them grind.

"But you've done so much for me. Been so nice," she

said softly, turning to look at him.

His doubled fists shook. "You think I'm so damn nice?"

"I know people. I can read people," she offered in an even voice, hoping to calm his rising anger.

"You think so, huh? Remember me?" he said, unfisting his right hand and pointing its thumb at his chest. "I was going to hock your ring."

Ida's eyes grew wide and she nibbled at her lower lip, not wanting him to go on but unable to speak.

"You listening?

"Let's just forget it," she offered in a meek voice.

"I wasn't bringing it back here. I was going to hock it. So stop trying to be so nice."

"You had to, though, didn't you? You had to protect your grandmother. That's no sin, Junior."

Raising both hands to press against his temples and looking down at the ground, he said in a shaky, angry voice, "It was a sin to me." And he walked away.

~*~

Ida continued her pruning, too shaken by Junior's response to give up and wanting to think about how she'd managed to offend him. She meant it well, but it had gone sour. She moved along the row of bushes, haphazardly chopping the rose hips from the stems, and looked back after a while to see she had a mess to clean up.

She was headed for the garage to find a rake rather than stoop down and use her hands when Eula came out of the guest house. Ida stopped and waited for the old woman to get near. She noticed that Eula no longer hobbled.

"Pruning?" Eula said.

"Yes. Junior was helping me clear out these borders."

Eula looked back at the guest house. "Huh. He must have gone in to use the bathroom. He'll be back. Once he starts something, he always finishes it."

"Are you comfortable here, Eula? Everything you need?"

"Why, yes. I can't... We can't thank you enough for taking us in. I don't know where we'd have gone."

"I owed that much to Junior. More really. But this I can do, and it makes me happy," Ida said, looking to make sure Junior hadn't come back out. "Does he really want to be doctor? I mean. Is he driven, do you think?"

Eula laughed. "That boy played doctor from the age of six. Used to wear one of my old house coats. White and turned up at the bottom with safety pins... Yes, he is driven. It's a good word for him. Driven."

"Will you be able to help him? It's none of my business, but medical school is quite costly."

Eula looked pained for a moment. "Not much, I guess. Only have my Social Security. No savings," she said, glancing down at her feet as if she were ashamed or at least sad about it. She looked back up quickly, though, and smiled. "He's smart, though. Gets scholarships. He'll make it happen."

"Yes. He is smart," Ida said, offering a warm, small smile. "He'll do it."

~*~

It was a dim light that came from the dated floor lamp with its rose-beige shade, not a light one could read by. Perhaps Arthur hadn't been a reader, Eula thought, as she telescoped her Bible, trying for enough light and yet needing a certain amount of distance to focus. But it was no use. There simply was no magic distance, so she closed it with a thump and set it on the hassock in front of her.

She heard Junior open the bathroom door as he brushed his teeth, having showered, and could smell the fresh chamomile scent of the soap he had used. She liked this place. She liked knowing that they were in a safe neighborhood, that good people were nearby, people she could talk to and look forward to seeing. Eula wanted to stay.

Her eyelids fluttered as she fell off the edge into one of the many unannounced naps that grew in number each day. Mae was there, seven and saucer-eyed, her black bushy hair pomaded and defeated into braids with great care, as they played *one-potato, two-potato* on the narrow front porch of their house on Central Avenue. She was such a happy child, eager and quick to learn. She could hear the slap-slap of Mae's little hands hitting her palms. She smiled in her sleep, mumbling *five-potato, six-potato, seven-potato, more.*

It was half an hour later, when Junior had dressed and straightened up the bathroom after the shower he'd taken to remove the grime and sweat of gardening, that he found her in the living room slumped in the big chair. He stood over her, thinking she was having a bad dream, unable to make out the words she mumbled in her sleep. Queen, he thought, and shook his head. He leaned down to touch her shoulder, rubbing it gently, and heard her little snort as he watched her blink away what he wrongly assumed was a nightmare.

Eula reached up with one hand, wiping nonexistent drool from the corner of her mouth with her index finger. When she was able to focus on Junior, she saw the same eyes, Mae's eyes from her dream, and smiled. "Nodded off," she said, noticing he had dressed and was wearing a lightweight jacket. "Going out?"

"You wanted me to get them a gift. Remember?"

"I said when we leave."

"Right."

"But we're not leaving. They haven't found him yet. Have they?" She hoped not.

"No. But it can't go on forever. Sooner or later they'll get him. Besides, I need to get out of here for a while."

"Is it safe to go out?"

"It's only four blocks. There are a couple of shops by the store we went to yesterday. Maybe I can find something there."

"Doesn't have to be much."

"Can't be too much, I only have eighty bucks."

"Soaps maybe," she said, still able to smell the chamomile. "Ladies always like nice soaps."

Junior walked to the door. "I won't be long."

"You like them, don't you?" she said.

"Yes, but don't go getting any ideas. I'm not going to be anyone's houseboy."

~*~

Cato looked at his Rolex, rubbing his palm across the crystal to remove a smear. 7:30, she should be settled in by now, he thought, flipping his cigarette butt out the window and across the parking lot. He knew she was straight now, clean, but she was his only contact on the inside and he was growing desperate. This thing hanging over his head was starting to cut into his business. He had to find Junior and fast. He had avoided the police, but he knew he had to end it or his territory would soon be taken over by others. Word was already out that Queen had stiffed him again. It wouldn't be long before he was challenged, knowing the police were on his butt. He turned off the engine, the motor sputtering to a delayed stop as the dirty spark plugs continued to ignite the residual gas, and got out. He hated the Chrysler and knew he'd have to replace it soon.

The main entrance was too well lit to suit him, so he made his way around the side of the hospital, finding a half-closed door and going in. A call to a mutual friend had told him he'd find her on the fourth floor, and he climbed a deserted inner stairwell.

Looking through the 4/6" window, he saw her sitting behind the nurses' station, a doctor stood in front of her reviewing a chart and making notes. Asking around had paid off, he thought she'd left town a long time ago.

Whatever the doctor said must have been funny because Betty laughed as he walked away. He glanced both ways through the window, seeing the coast was clear, and entered the corridor.

"Hey, sweet woman. What's up?" he said, leaning on the counter and smiling.

Betty glanced up from her computer screen to see Cato's menacing smile. Her eyes darted, making sure no one was near. "What are you doing here?"

"Came to wish an old friend Merry Christmas, sweetheart," he said, seeing she was agitated.

"Leave me alone, Cato," she said, getting up and walking backwards toward a glassed-in room. "Trying to get me fired?"

Cato rounded the counter and followed her. "Need a little favor, baby," he said, backing her into the room.

"I'm not your baby. I'm off that stuff."

"So I hear. So I hear," he said, moving closer. "It's a good thing, too, 'cause a friend of mine told me hospitals are real touchy about who handles medications and such."

"Stay away from me. I'm not buying any stuff," she said, feeling his threat.

"I ain't selling, baby. I'm buying."

Betty pushed past him and walked out of the room. Cato turned slowly and went after her.

"I'll call security."

"No. I don't think you will. 'Less, of course, you'd like me to talk with them. Lots I could tell them."

"What do you want?"

"Just a little billing information. Release forms, maybe," he smiled. "I could be out of here just like that," he said, snapping his big fingers in the air.

CHAPTER TWENTY-FIVE

Madeline reached high for the crockery mixing bowl, fumbling it forward on the top shelf with one hand and holding onto the cabinet door with the other. She couldn't quite reach the rim for a firm grip. It had been a bad night for her. Dreams of Billy Lee and Sukie and train whistles had troubled her sleep, leaving her tired this morning of all mornings. There was so much to do, she thought as she worried the bowl in a circle with her fingertips. When the bowl finally did walk forward, it did so too fast, and her big black hand failed to stop it in time. It fell to the countertop, making at first a hollow thump of a sound followed by an ear-piercing shatter, scattering shards in every direction.

Madeline issued an oath of protest but knew she was to blame and not the bowl. She should have used the step stool. She shrugged a little and closed the cabinet door, stepping cautiously through the shards. She took her broom and dustpan and swept the widely strewn pieces of her favorite mixing bowl together, stooping to gather them up and dumping them into the wastebasket. There was too much to get done today if she wanted tomorrow's dinner to be relatively peaceful for her.

"Let it go, Madeline," she said softly as she made her way to the back pantry to retrieve one of the less satisfying but serviceable aluminum mixing bowls. It wasn't often that this old disappointment came back to haunt her. It usually happened when she was feeling that life was passing her by, that she'd missed her chance. "What ifs. Ain't," she said to herself. It was a little phrase her mother used to use and one that helped clear the air for her sometimes.

The metal measuring cup clicked against the side of the bowl four times as she dumped in the level cups of flour. She took four eggs from the carton, cracking them one at a time into the mound of flour, as the "what ifs" refused to be ignored. It was always the things that hadn't happened that bothered Madeline. Those that had never troubled her, not even her brief encounter with Billy Lee on the church pew. She had no regrets about that or about spending most of her life as a housekeeper. While she regretted Billy Lee not coming back for her, she knew he would not have stuck by her for long. Sukie had written about him a few years after she'd left Peoria, telling how he'd moved from one woman to another, how he'd been in and out of prison and died of a heroin overdose. What she regretted was not having been pregnant, not having children. She could never have trusted Billy Lee, but she could have had a child. And she regretted not having been there for the march on Washington with Dr. King, not having carried a banner and not hearing his famous speech. She should have done it. She'd had the money and could have done it. Ida had even asked her whether she wanted to go or not.

From the hallway above, she heard the creaking planks and knew that Ida had been woken by the crashing bowl. She splattered some milk atop the other ingredients and began to beat the batter. "What ifs.

~ 154 ~

Ain't," she said.

The morning sun bounced about the shiny surfaces of the spotless kitchen, squinting Ida's eyes as she entered. The steady, hollow *clop-clop-clop* of the wooden spoon hitting the batter reminded Ida of riding her horse Lulu down the then-unpaved lanes of Evanston. The rhythm and the duration of the beating said a lot about Madeline. I'd have called it quits long ago, she thought. Was she beating or grinding an axe? She'd been awfully quiet since breakfast yesterday, before that even.

"Heard a crash," Ida said, making her way to the coffee pot. "What broke."

"Nothing."

"Sounded like something."

"Nothing important."

"Coffee," Ida offered, noticing the edge Madeline wore so plainly.

"Don't have time... You drink too much of that stuff, anyway."

"Okay. What is it?" Ida asked. "What's eating you?"

"Eating me. Nothing's eating me," Madeline said, continuing to beat the mixture, her expression sour.

"Oh, yes. Something's eating you. Let's have it."

Madeline glanced at Ida, and she increased her speed. "You want them to stay," she said, glancing again. "Working on them. I've got eyes."

"And what's the matter with that? I thought you liked Eula?"

"I do like Eula," she said, looking squarely at Ida. "What I know of her."

"What you know? And Junior?"

Madeline shrugged and she stopped beating. "You're too naive about people like that."

"People like what?"

"You know what I mean."

"No. No, I don't know what you mean."

"His mother's a drug addict and a prostitute.

Probably didn't know who the father was," Madeline said, setting her jaw. "Name like Junior," she made a little humphing noise.

Ida knew the look. *Made-up-my-mind.* "Contagious, you think?"

"Blood tells."

"That's Peoria talking again."

"Left Peoria years ago."

"Are you sure about that?"

Madeline ignored her comment. "You need to be more careful who you trust."

"I'm a good judge of character," Ida said, incensed.

"I'm just saying go slow. I don't want anyone to get hurt," Madeline said, beginning to stroke the batter again.

"Are you jealous?"

Madeline pursed her lips and shook her head, the beating turned furious. Ida watched, knowing she'd done it again.

"Sorry I said that," Ida said, drawing closer to Madeline and putting her hand on her shoulder as Madeline's beating subsided to a steady pace. "I know you're only looking out for me."

The phone rang and Ida walked to answer it. "And I appreciate that. I do," she said, picking up the receiver. "Hello... Hello, is anyone there?" She heard the click on the other end of the line and hung up.

~*~

The white undercloth snapped in the air and floated into place on the highly polished surface of the mahogany dining table. Madeline smoothed out the creases and lifted the lace tablecloth from the back of the armchair, placing it dead center, hoping to unfold it without wrinkling the base.

Junior pushed the swinging door open enough to stick his head in. "Need help?"

Madeline was glad to hear the words. There was just too much to get done today. She didn't want the little things to interfere with tomorrow's day of last minute cooking. But when she looked into his eyes, she saw Billy Lee again and hesitated. She knew it was unfair, knew he meant well. "Yes, thank you," she said, pointing to the other side of the table, and tried without much luck to muster a smile. "Grab the other side, would you?"

Junior followed Madeline's lead, unfolding the cloth and settling it into place carefully. When it was done, Madeline bent down to see that it was even all the way around the table, tugging slightly on one side. "There," she said and walked to the sideboard, opening the middle drawer and taking out several silver serving pieces. "Now, look at that," she said, shaking her head at the tarnish. "Tell you what. You set the table," she said, opening the china closet. "Blue and white china on the bottom. Flatware and napkins in the drawers, the red plaid ones."

"Under control," he said, lifting a stack of china as Madeline went to the kitchen to polish the silver. He counted out five of the plates and walked around the table, setting two at the ends, two on one side and one on the other. He lifted the extra chair from the back and placed it against the wall next to the sideboard.

When Madeline returned, Junior had placed the napkins around the table and was busy distributing the flatware. Madeline smiled weakly, seeing how evenly he had placed everything. She looked up as Ida came to the double French doors, stopping to watch Junior who didn't notice her. It was then that Madeline saw the five place settings.

"Five?" she said, wrinkling her brow. "We only need four."

Junior continued to place the flatware. "There's you, me, Grandma, Ida and her son. Right?" he said, not looking up.

Madeline looked at Ida, seeing the pain. Ida returned her glance and shook her head no. "He's... well... of course. Yes, fine. Five," Madeline said as the phone rang in the background.

Ida turned away from the doors and went to answer the phone. "Hello... Hello..." she said, but the line went dead. Again, she thought.

The doorbell rang, momentarily confusing Ida, who picked up the receiver and set it back down.

~*~

It was the side of the black woman's face Ida saw when she opened the door, giving her the opportunity to see the dark circles behind the large white-framed sunglasses. When she turned to face Ida, there was something familiar about her. Ida couldn't quite name it.

"I'm looking for my son," Queen said.

"Your son?" Ida said, tilting her head and recognizing the jaw line and proud posture. "Junior?"

"That's right. And my mother," Queen said, reaching up to pat down her errant hair, knowing she looked unkempt and feeling more so in Ida's tidy presence.

"Why, yes," Ida said, backing up and opening the door wide. "I'll get him. Do come in."

"Best not," she said, looking down at her feet.

"I see. Well, one minute."

Queen licked her lips and ran a hand over her stomach, trying to smooth the wrinkles from her black dress. She hoped it would be her mother who came to the door.

Junior stepped around the open door already armed with a scowl, but it was a shock to see her looking so bad; no makeup, the yellow cast of her unpolished nails, a plain dress that went to mid-calf, and flat shoes.

"What do you want?" he said.

"I heard what happened. I... I came to make sure

you're okay."

"Yeah. Sure," Junior said, rolling his eyes. He stepped out onto the porch and closed the door behind him. Just inside the door, Ida and Madeline drew closer to listen. "Sure you did."

"Don't start, Junior. I may not be much, but..."

"Got that right," he interrupted.

Queen lifted her sunglasses, poking them down into her hair and letting them rest atop her head. "But I am your mother. I was worried."

"Thought you'd be in Vegas by now. Run out of money?"

"I didn't go to Vegas. I went to Preston House."

"What's that? A whorehouse?"

Queen narrowed her eyes, her nostrils flaring slightly. "Rehab. I went to rehab," she said, suppressing the "smartass" she felt like adding.

Junior was stunned for a moment, not knowing how to respond. But not so stunned that he let his defenses down. "How did you find us?"

"Mr. Burke. I went home. Locks are changed," she said, looking away from his stare. "He gave me her name. Only one in the book."

"He shouldn't have."

Queen winced and blew a long sigh, making a barely noticeable whooshing noise. "How's Momma?"

"She's okay," he said, watching as she turned back and forced a little smile. "So now, we have no apartment, huh? Make you happy?"

She lifted her hands to her temples and rubbed them in circles, the headache in its fourth day. "Stop this, Junior. I... I'm trying."

He looked away from her, a part of him wanting to believe her, and swallowed the lump in his throat. "You want to see Gramma?" he said.

She stopped rubbing her head and nodded, pulling the sunglasses back into place.

"Round back," he said, pointing to the driveway.

Junior walked down the steps ahead of her, leading her around the side of the house. She followed at a safe distance.

"She hasn't got any money," he said without looking back as he walked.

Queen shook her head, sucking in her lower lip but saying nothing. She stepped up her pace, determined not to let him beat her down.

When they reached the door to the guest house, Junior stopped and turned to face her. "Don't be asking for any money."

Queen looked up at the roof line over the door, avoiding his smug face. "You're a hard ass, aren't you?" she said, looking back down and pushing him to the side to reach the door.

"I wonder why?" he said and added, "Can't stay here, you know."

"Don't worry. I can't stay, anyway."

"They have you on methadone?"

"Just let me talk to Mamma, okay?" she said, opening the door and closing it behind her.

~*~

Ida and Madeline ducked to the sides of the kitchen window, not wanting to be caught eavesdropping on their conversation. Peeking around the corner of the window, Ida saw Junior go into the garage. She reached over and pulled the window down, gritting her teeth as it scraped against the fame.

"She looks bad," Ida said.

"Now what are you going to do?" Madeline said, her arms crossed beneath her large breasts.

"Do? Do about what?"

"She can't stay here. Can't have drug addicts and prostitutes here."

Ida raised both hands, pumping them in the air in

front of her, warning Madeline to back off. "I know. I know," she said, walking back to the kitchen table and taking a seat. She took a sip of her coffee and made a face, surprised it had gone cold.

Madeline came to stand in front of her. "Have you asked them to stay?" she said, her arms still signaling an immovable force.

Ida glanced up and then back to her cold coffee. She rotated the cup slowly with the fingers of both hands. "Well... yes. Yes, I have mentioned it."

Madeline shook her head, "What did I tell you? Said go slow. Go slow, didn't I?"

"Mae hasn't asked to stay," Ida pointed out, her eyes still avoiding Madeline.

"Not yet. She will. You heard her say they're locked out. Where else does she have to go? Where else do any of them have to go?"

"All right, Madeline," Ida said and stopped fidgeting with her cup, raising one hand to rub the back of her neck. "All right. That's enough. I have to think."

Madeline didn't like being dismissed, not when the topic affected her just as much as it did Ida. "Just have to uninvite them," she mumbled as she went back to the sink.

CHAPTER TWENTY-SIX

They're not her eyes, not the same eyes, Eula thought, staring into their blankness. It was her daughter, all right. It was Mae. But someone had switched her eyes. Someone or something had stolen the life right out of her, taking it through her eyes and leaving nothing but wounds.

Queen sat on the edge of her mother's new bed, looking around at the strange but homey surroundings as they talked. She wished her mother could stay here, that Junior could stay, but she knew that was too much to ask. It was all her fault. She knew that. She had counted on Cato's supposed fondness for her to keep him from harming them. He hadn't the last time, and even though he'd warned her, she thought he still cared enough not to do anything to them. She should have known better.

"I know you're trying, baby."

"That damn Cato. His own son?" Queen said, curling her lip and shaking her head.

"Shush. Junior could hear you," Eula said.

"Maybe he should. So cocky. Thinks he's so damn smart."

"He is smart."

"Hates me."

"He's never to know. We agreed. Never," Eula said, taking her daughter's hand. "He's got chances. Chances you and I never had." She could feel a vibration transmitted through her daughter's hand. Nerves?, she wondered. "You didn't tell Cato about him? He still doesn't know?" Eula wanted no part of Cato laying claim on Junior as his son.

"No," she answered softly. "He'll never know." Eula's hand was warm in hers, and she looked away, squeezing it. "I haven't been good, Momma. I know that. But I'm trying to straighten up," she said, turning back to Eula. "I am trying."

"I'm praying for you, baby."

Queen leaned over and gave her a firm hug, saying softly in her ear, "Gotta go back. They don't like us out after dark." She stood up, releasing her tight hold on her mother and walking to the bedroom door. "I'm sorry about all this."

"I know," Eula said.

"Pray for me, Mamma."

"I am, baby. Merry Christmas."

"Merry Christmas. Humph, yeah."

Eula watched her leave, continuing to stare into the blank space of the doorway, hoping they'd give her eyes back.

~*~

The Venetian blind on the door window rattled and Junior pushed away from the wall he was leaning against, kneeling quickly, pretending to be weeding the border along the front of the guest house. He looked up to see her pulling her sunglasses back into position as she closed the door behind her. She looked over and saw him rise.

"I... I couldn't tell you where I was going. Could I?

Queen said, looking away from him. "I mean. Cato and all."

"That right?" Junior said, frowning in disbelief. "Could have asked for the money?"

Queen turned her sad eyes back to him. "Would you have given it to me?" But Junior didn't answer her. "Never mind," she said.

"How will you get back?" he asked, brushing his hands against the sides of his slacks.

"Bus."

He fished a ten-dollar bill from his pocket, his last one, and held it out to her. "Take this. Get a cab."

Queen stared at the bill, glancing between it and Junior's clear brown eyes. "No, thanks. Guess I've taken enough."

"Call it a Christmas present," he said, lifting her hand and forcing it to close around the bill.

She drew her hand away, looking at her fist and swallowed hard. "Thanks... Thanks, you hear?"

"Yeah... sure."

~*~

As Queen passed by the front porch making her way down the driveway to the sidewalk, Ida stepped from behind the oleander bush. "Excuse me," she said.

Queen stared at her for a moment, thinking she must have been watching for some time and wondering how much she knew. "Yes," she said, not risking a smile.

"It's just that.... well, I wondered, if you can find them, can this Cato?"

"No. Mr. Burke didn't tell him where they were. I think you're safe," she said, starting to walk again. When she reached the sidewalk, she turned back, seeing Ida watching her. "Thanks for taking them in. I appreciate it," she said, offering a weak smile.

"It's no trouble," she said, smiling back. "I like them,

you know?"

"Good. It's a load off my mind."

"Your Junior's a smart boy. He'll be something someday. Deserves a break," Ida said, finding herself rambling as she watched Queen backing down the sidewalk.

"Yeah. He does," she said, turning to pick up her pace and mumbling to herself. "We all do."

~*~

Junior found Madeline and Ida in the kitchen. He had the feeling they were waiting for him. He sensed Madeline's uneasiness, watching her pick up a dishtowel and wipe at the counter as she gave Ida a prodding eye.

"Sorry she showed up. I didn't think she could find us," he said, hoping it would unleash whatever they wanted to talk to him about.

"Don't be sorry," Ida said. "Eula's probably glad to know she's okay."

"Okay?" he said with half a laugh. "Wouldn't exactly call rehab okay."

"Rehab? Really? Why, that's a good sign," Ida said, but Junior didn't answer.

Madeline set the towel aside and walked to the dining room door. "I've got things to do," she said, nodding to Ida, reminding her it was time to talk to him and leaving the room.

"You do think she can make it, don't you?" Ida asked.

"No. Probably not," he said, walking to the window and looking out. He was quiet for a minute and then said, "We're not staying, you know? You don't need to worry about us staying on here," he said, guessing Queen's arrival had the old women worrying. "Okay?"

Ida was both stunned and relieved, and yet profoundly disappointed. "Why?"

"With Queen trying to... well, it just wouldn't work. Besides, we never wanted to stay in the first place."

"It's a bit of a problem, I admit. But..." she began.

"No, don't," he said, turning to look at her. "Hey, you've done enough."

Ida watched him walk to the back door and open it. "It's not that I wouldn't like to try. I mean..."

"We'll be just fine. Don't worry. We can take care of ourselves," he said, leaving and closing the door behind him.

Ida's stomach was churning. She raised her hand to her forehead and rubbed it, hearing the squeak of the swinging door behind her. She turned to see Madeline standing there.

"Don't say it," she warned Madeline, who took on a hurt expression.

"I wasn't going to say anything."

"Yes you were. You did the right thing. That's what you were going to say."

"Well, you did. Didn't you?" Madeline said, wondering if it really had been the right thing herself.

"Did I?"

"I hope so," Madeline said, feeling hollow and regretting her own advice.

~*~

The late afternoon sun played among the high-rises, peering over some and flashing between others, blinding Cato in a game of hide and seek as he drove along Wilshire Boulevard, holding his left hand six inches from his forehead, glancing up to scowl at the space where the missing sun visor should have been. "Shit," he mumbled, the shielding hand nearly causing him to miss the street sign. He hit the brakes, turning right into the neighborhood of huge homes, clean streets and manicured lawns.

The engine sputtered as he gave it a little gas. His

latest trip to the LAX Auto Mart was a bigger disappointment than the Chrysler had been, but he'd been in a hurry. The jerk he'd seen schlepping his three bags didn't know how to take care of a car. The outside looked great. The inside of the Jeep Cherokee was pretty funky, but he hadn't noticed the missing visor. It was time, though. He knew better than to hold onto the Chrysler for too long.

He slowed to a crawl, watching ahead for any sign of an unmarked car, looking both ways at each cross street. When he reach the 300 block, he began to scan the house numbers, knowing it would be on the left side of the street.

No one was parked on the right side of the street, so he eased to the curb, seeing the house number, stopping momentarily and thinking the old house needed a coat of paint. He could see the Christmas tree in the window. He released his left foot from the brake, allowing the car to float forward. Looking down the long driveway, his eyes grew larger and he smiled to himself, touching the brake pedal once again.

Junior was dragging an overstuffed, black plastic bag past the open garage doors headed for two trash barrels. He had a rusty rake in his other hand, and he glanced over at Cato's car, but not recognizing it, continued his march to the barrels.

Cato drove slowly to the end of the block, intending to turn around for another pass. He caught the massive grill of the Ford in his rear view mirror when he reached the corner and instinct told him to duck. He turned right, careful not to accelerate and draw attention, and pulled into the driveway of the first house beside a Lincoln Town Car.

Shielded by the huge sedan, he stared through the three sets of windows, seeing the patrol car do a U-turn at the corner and then disappear.

~*~

Dawkins pulled to the curb and put the car in park, waiting on the side street in Compton as Jimmy had directed. Warren was busy with her notebook as usual, and he frowned, slouching down and getting comfortable. At least she wasn't talking, he thought.

Warren pressed a period mark hard, too hard, and the pencil snapped. She glanced at Dawkins, who offered a weak smile and fished around in her tiny purse for another pencil. She hated the tiny purse, only purchasing it with the thought that it wasn't obvious. It didn't look so much like a handbag. Finding no pencil or even a pen, she reached over and punched the glove box button. It dropped open, and at about the same time, Dawkins sat up taking hold of the steering wheel. The cellophane wrapper on the package of cigarettes gleamed out at her. She turned her head to look at Dawkins.

"What's this? Thought you were quitting."

Dawkins tried to look nonchalant. "Insurance. It's not open. Look for yourself."

Warren lifted it out, calling his bluff. Sure enough, hadn't been opened. She tossed it back in and took out a pen.

After a few minutes, a new black BMW pulled in behind them and Jimmy got out. He scanned the area nervously and approached their car. He'd deliberately picked Compton because few people here would recognize him. He worked the Southwest side and seldom ventured east of the Harbor Freeway. He opened the back door and slid in behind Warren and Dawkins, leaning forward to talk over the seat.

"Hey, Dawk," he said, using the short name Dawkins hated. "Who's the lady?"

"I'm no lady, asshole," Warren said, deciding to get off on the right foot with this ex-con street louse.

Dawkins laughed, mentally chalking up the first and only point he'd given her so far.

"Whoa, Mamma. Got some attitude there."

"She's with me now. Go easy on her."

Jimmy shrugged. "What's goin' down?"

"Need a little favor," said Dawkins.

"Oh, man. Haven't you used up my debts yet?"

Dawkins ignored him, knowing he had enough information on Jimmy to make him a target. "Know Cato Hobbs?"

"Cato. Sure. Works the Slauson corridor. Mean."

"That's the one. Want you to put the word out he's washed up. His territory is up for grabs."

"Shit," Jimmy spat out, shaking his skinny head. "Like to see my ass dead, man? Messin' with dealers."

"Your choice."

"Shit," he said again, opening the door and slamming it shut. He mumbled to himself as he walked away.

"Well?" Warren said, thinking he'd refused.

"Well what?"

"Anybody else in mind?"

Dawkins chuckled to himself and started the engine. "He'll do it."

CHAPTER TWENTY-SEVEN

The colored lights of the Christmas tree in the bay window offered the only light in the room, and Madeline almost missed Ida, standing next to it looking out at the clear moonlit night.

"Everything's ready for tomorrow," she said, waiting for Ida to respond. "Just a salad for dinner tonight." She could see Ida's eyes in the reflection on the glass as they glanced up to take note of her old friend, but Ida didn't say a thing. "Are you listening?" she asked softly, tilting her head, wondering what thoughts were hiding behind Ida's lost expression.

"Where is the shotgun?" Ida said, breaking her silence.

"Shotgun?"

"Yes, where is it?" Ida said, her voice edgy.

"Back of the hall closet. Why?"

"Is it loaded?"

"I guess so. But why?"

Ida turned around and walked past Madeline without answering and entered the hallway. Madeline followed, watching her open the closet door and forage behind the hanging coats. Ida took the shotgun out and leaned it against the hall table in front of her son's silver-framed photograph, then closed the closet door.

Madeline came closer, looking worried. "What's that for?"

"Protection," Ida said, hefting the shotgun to her hip and struggling to break it down. The two brass circles were visible, so Ida snapped the shotgun closed, making a cracking noise.

"I don't like this," Madeline said, locking her arms under her breasts. "Don't like this one bit."

Ida looked up at her. "Neither do I," she said, carrying the shotgun to the front door and leaning it against the wall. She lifted the curtain on the window next to the door and saw a patrol car drive slowly past.

"Why did you let Junior think he was coming to dinner?" Madeline asked, watching Ida's head turn away from the window.

"Why? Because I don't need sympathy. That's why."

~*~

Madeline heard the grandfather's clock strike ten as she checked to see that the deadbolt was in place and switched off the front porch light. Ten past ten, she thought, knowing the old clock to be ten minutes slow. She yawned, walked across the hall and entered the living room, her legs aching from her busy day of preparation.

Crossing to the bay window, she bent slightly and pulled the plug from the wall socket, dousing the tree lights and sending the big room into darkness. She straightened up and hesitated for a moment, allowing the visual purple of her night vision to take hold. As her eyes began to focus, she heard a click and scanned the room, not seeing anything. Through the open dining room doors, she noticed a movement. She craned her head, seeing the dark profile in the window against the background of the moonlit back yard, and her heart began to race.

Holding one hand to her breast and using the other to fend off the unknown like a blind man, she crept slowly across the room and reached around the corner to switch on the chandelier over the gaily set table.

"Leave that off!" Ida barked.

Madeline exhaled slowly and took a deep breath of safe air. "What is this?" she asked.

"This is an old lady protecting her property," she said, gruffly. "Now shut that off!"

"Protecting it from what?" Madeline said, switching off the light.

"From a murderer."

"You can't be serious?" Madeline said, walking to the window and seeing the garage and guest house flooded with moonlight and the shotgun resting against the wall between the windows.

"I am. 'Til they catch him, I'm responsible."

"But the police are watching the house."

"Driving by every so often. It's not enough."

"He can't possibly know they're here."

"We had three hang-up calls today."

"Wrong number. Happens all the time."

"No it doesn't."

"Come to bed. It's late. You'll have a full day tomorrow."

Ida looked up at her with a frustrated expression. "No. Go to bed."

Madeline knew better than to argue with Ida. "Suit yourself," she said and made her way out, looking back at Ida's profile and shaking her head.

~*~

Junior leaned in the doorway and Eula glanced up from her open Bible. "Got a bad feeling," she said.

He crossed the room and sat on the edge of the bed. "That right? About what?"

"Just a feeling. Wish they'd catch him."

"Me, too. We could move on."

"Move on? Where?"

"Have to see Mr. Raymond. Get the place back."

Eula looked down at the book. "We don't have to, you know? Don't have to leave."

Junior stared at her, waiting for her to look up. When she did, he asked, "Has she been talking to you?"

Eula saw his lips purse and his eyes narrow. "Now, don't go getting that look."

"Gramma, you don't understand."

"Yes, I do," she said, taking his right hand. "You don't take charity, and that's admirable."

Junior pulled his hand free and held it in the palm of his left one, looking at the dirt he'd failed to scrub from under his nails. "It's not just that. She's having second thoughts, too. Thinks Queen's part of the package."

"Did she say that?"

"I could see it. I let her off the hook, though," he said, releasing his hand and giving it back to his grandmother. "Besides, haven't we always got by? Just you and me."

"Got by? Yes, I guess. If that's all there is to life, getting by."

"I don't want to end up being a houseboy. End up like Madeline."

"Why, Junior Thomas, shame on you. Madeline is a fine woman."

"I don't mean that. I know she's okay. It's just that I want something more," he said, getting up and walking over to look out the window. "I just want everything back to normal. Just you and me taking care of ourselves. No Queen. No Cato. Just us."

Eula winced, gripping her Bible and pulling it to her chest. It was painful to hear him exclude her baby from their future.

She watched him turn and make his way to the door

and wondered if his prayers ever included his mother.

"Night, Gramma," he said, turning to look at her.

She stared into his eyes, seeing her daughter's eyes, and said, "Night, Junior. Night baby."

CHAPTER TWENTY-EIGHT

The headlights dipped as the patrol car crossed the spillway running through the intersection and cruised slowly down Hudson. Cato heard the pop of the rock being spit from under the huge tire and the subsequent clacking as it ricocheted along the curb. It was the fourth patrol since taking up his watch. He checked his Rolex, figuring that they averaged twenty minutes apart. Plenty of time, he thought. He got out of the car, pulling on his black stocking cap. He knew it had to be tonight. Calvin, his primary runner, had been suspiciously surprised to see him. He didn't know who put the word out, but he knew he had only a day or two before his turf would be history.

The full moon offered too much light for him to safely use the sidewalk even with the overhanging oak trees, so he walked across the lawns, staying close to the houses. He kept an eye out for headlights from either direction and spotted safe places to duck as he moved along should the need arise. He knew he couldn't take any chances on being seen.

When he reached the driveway, he looked both ways to make sure the patrol car hadn't doubled back for any reason. As he moved from window to window along the side of the house, he pushed up on them, hoping someone had left one unlocked. He carried a crowbar hooked on his belt if needed, but he preferred a less-noisy entrance. They were all locked or perhaps painted shut, he thought. Rounding the corner at the end of the driveway, he saw the single yellow bulb shining over the door to the guest house and smiled.

Cato was halfway across the open yard when he heard the grandfather's clock strike one through the open dining room window. He could see the lower half of the window had been raised ten inches, but it was so dark in the house that he couldn't see Ida slumped against the inner frame, her head flopped down onto her chest and one hand hanging limply to her side. He looked over at the guest house and then back to the open window, deciding to eliminate the smaller area first.

He took his hat off and used it to unscrew the light bulb, fighting off the five or six gnats that death-danced about it. He leaned against the door, pressing his ear to the glass before trying the handle, and hearing nothing from within, he tried turning the handle but found it was locked.

Maxwell's ears perked at the first muted cracking of the splintering wood. He gave a low set of growls and climbed to his feet, ambling to the fence, straining to hear more, growling again. Cato looked back from the door, relieved the tall fence separated him from the dog and its fierce, low-pitched growl. He knew it would take another effort to break the door from the frame and hoped the dog wouldn't bark. He coiled the stocking cap around the crowbar where it met the door frame, hoping to muffle the sound, and gave a strong yank. The door gave way, making a loud crack despite his attempt to mute it. Maxwell barked several times before stopping to listen, unable to make out what was taking place beyond his fence. Cato stood still.

Madeline's eyes flickered at first, hearing Maxwell's call. She rolled over, punching the pillow and heaving a sigh.

Junior had tossed in his bed at the same time the crack sounded, freezing him momentarily. He strained to listen, wondering if it was the bed frame that had made the noise. Why was the neighbor's dog barking, he thought, throwing back the covers and rising on one elbow.

Ida was still fast asleep.

It was dark in the little living room after the bright moonlight outside. Cato took the penlight from his pocket, switching it on and shining its narrow light around the room at first and then along the floor ahead of him. He turned slowly the handle of the first door in the short hallway, easing it open without releasing the knob. He saw the pink bathrobe draped across the foot of the bed and sniffed the air, recognizing the smell of Noxzema and realizing it was Eula's room. He pulled the door closed and walked to the next one. The door was ajar, so he lightly pushed it with his right hand, trying to focus without shining the penlight into the room. He stepped in, squinting in the direction of the bed. He took another step, kicking a stray shoe across the room, before flashing the compact beam of light in Junior's panic-stricken face.

Junior leaped from the bed, butting Cato in the chest with his head and sending him stumbling backward over a chair, the noise setting off Maxwell once again. He was out of the room and down the hall by the time Cato caught up with him. Cato's huge sweaty hand reached around in front of him as he ran and clamped down on his face, the nails digging into his flesh and distorting its features. With one yank, Cato sent Junior slamming to the floor on his back and knocking the wind from him. Junior rolled to his right, running into the sofa and dug his hands into the cushions, struggling to get to his feet.

Cato fumbled about in the dark and found Junior's right foot. He stood quickly and twisted in a half circle, pulling Junior by one foot into the air as if using him to bat a high fly ball. Junior hit Arthur's favorite winged-back chair, sending it toppling, as Cato let go of his hold. Cato reached down to pull up his pant leg and withdrew the buck knife. He could hear Eula calling in terror to her grandson from the bedroom. Make it fast, he thought, fast and out before she could see him. He hated the idea of having to kill the old woman. He stepped forward and leaned down.

The two blasts of the shotgun rattled the windows and echoed through the back yard. Eula's screams were drowned out by Maxwell barking with added furor as Ida raced down the back steps just in time to see headlights flood the driveway and the patrol car screech to a stop in front of her, the red lights flashing and bouncing off the garage and guest house.

Two young officers jumped from the car wielding rifles. Ida pointed to the open door of the guest house just as Madeline walked out, the shotgun hanging loosely in one hand and the other clutching her stomach. Ida's arm shot out in front of the officers, signaling them to hold off, fearing they'd mistake Madeline for dangerous.

"In there," Madeline said to the officers. "Better call an ambulance." She dropped the shotgun and sat down on the ground.

Ida raced to her side, kneeling and taking her hand. "Junior?" she asked.

"He's okay. Cato will need a lot of work, though," she said, turning her attention to the police. "Junior's holding him down, but he really can't go anywhere."

The officers raced past them and into the guest house. Madeline was shaking violently and Ida sat down next to her, pulling her close and stroking her hair.

"Never shot anyone before," she said, her hands folded around her stomach, holding it in as if something were trying to escape from deep inside.

"You did it for me, didn't you?"

"No," Madeline said, rocking slowly in Ida's arms. "No, for Junior... For me."

~*~

Detective Warren pounded the steering wheel of her Honda with her fists as she sat at the long traffic light. "Shit. Shit. Shit," she mumbled under her breath. She wanted to turn on the siren and slap the hidden red light on the dash, but knew it was against policy unless a true emergency warranted it, with everything under control there'd be no excuse. When the light finally changed to green, she pressed hard on the gas pedal, squealing the tires as she flew forward along Wilshire Boulevard. She'd risk being pulled over, she thought, that much she'd risk.

Of all the nights he would call her, she would have had three glasses of wine. "Shit," she said again, seeing the traffic light on the corner of Hudson coming into view and slowing her pace for the turn. She hoped this was a good sign. That perhaps he was beginning to trust her.

As she turned onto Hudson, she reached over to dig in her purse and pull out a roll of mints, using her nails to blindly free one of them.

~*~

Junior held the cold pack against his forehead, resting his head on the back of the sofa. Eula sat next to him with her Bible still clutched in one hand as Dawkins came in from the back yard, followed by Warren who jotted notes on her pad as she walked. The flickering red flashes of the patrol car lights painted the room with the eerie light of a cheap motel room facing an overactive neon sign. Dawkins went back to the door, shaking his head.

"Cut the goddamn lights," he yelled at the two officers and turned back to see Eula holding her Bible. "Ah, sorry, ma'am," he said but Eula hadn't heard it.

"Excuse me," Ida said from behind him, wanting to enter but blocked out.

He took two more steps forward, letting her pass. "He'll live," he said, referring to Cato.

"Good," Ida said, taking a seat in the recently up-righted high-back chair. "Madeline will be relieved. They gave her a sedative. She's asleep."

"Taking him for stomach surgery," he added, watching Ida get up and go to the windows to stare out. Must be too nervous to sit, he thought. Should have taken a pill herself.

Warren flipped her notepad closed and clicked the ballpoint, causing Ida to glance up at her. When Warren smiled at her, she turned back to continue staring numbly out the window without returning it. Warren wondered how she could bridge their gap. How do you tell someone you're sorry for calling their old things old?

Dawkins walked over to Junior's side, glancing back to make sure Ida was not watching, and extended his cupped right hand to Junior. Warren watched him, wrinkling her brow and wondering what he was up to. "Ahem," Dawkins said, clearing his voice quietly to get Junior's attention, not wanting Ida to know what he was doing.

Junior looked at Dawkins and then to his extended hand. He reached up and felt the metal ring drop into his palm, still warm from the detective's grip. Dawkins nodded toward Ida's back and flashed his eyes before backing away. For the first time that Dawkins could remember, he saw Junior smile.

"What..." Eula started to ask but saw Dawkins raise

one finger to his lips, shushing her. It was then that Warren knew she had a chance with him.

"Mrs. Hanson," Junior said and watched as Ida's head swiveled quickly at the uncharacteristically formal address. He signaled for her to approach by waving the fist that held the ring, still pressing the cold pack to his brow.

"Mrs. Hanson?" she said, crossing the room. "Since when am I Mrs. Hanson?"

Junior extended his hand to her, opening it slowly. "Since this," he said.

Ida hesitated, looking at the ring but not wanting to take it. She looked into Junior's face and saw the broad smile and knew she had to. She smiled back at him and took the ring, sliding it onto her finger and praying that it wouldn't be the beginning of the end.

"That the famous ring?" Dawkins said, stepping forward as if he'd never seen it and taking Ida's hand. "Very nice. We'll need it as evidence, though."

~*~

Warren made her way down the driveway, forced into the oleander bushes by the poorly parked patrol car. She stopped at the front of the house to brush the leaves and dust from her suit jacket and ran her hand through her hair.

She looked toward the street where Dawkins' unmarked car sat by the curb and wondered where he was. She'd seen him walking down the driveway a moment ago, but he was nowhere in sight. A puff of smoke wafted its way up from behind a big oak tree, and she frowned. She went to check it out.

Dawkins leaned against the trunk of the old tree, his head resting against the deeply grooved bark. He took another drag as Warren stepped into his view.

"Thought you quit?"

"A weak man," he said, taking another drag and

puffing the smoke out over his extended tongue in small, perfectly formed circles. "Or so my ex-wife says, anyway."

Warren smiled to herself and stepped a little closer. "Give me one of those," she said, offering him a rather gruff expression he'd couldn't read.

Dawkins pulled the pack from his pocket and shook out a cigarette. "I thought you didn't approved of smoking?" He said, offering it to her and preparing to light it. Warren took the cigarette, leaning forward, hearing the click of the lighter and inhaling a short puff.

"I don't," she said as she coughed softly and smiled.

CHAPTER TWENTY-NINE

Madeline was up with the sun. It wasn't that she felt rested, quite the contrary. The sleeping pills had worked, calming her shattered nerves and rendering her lifeless, but she found herself trudging through what seemed more like an endless journey than a night of rest, simultaneously fitful and weighted down. She had never taken anything to help her sleep before and decided that once was enough.

Even though she was still tired, getting out of bed was preferable to falling back into the muck-like realm she'd experienced. Besides, if dinner was to be ready by 4:00, she had lots to do.

She rose quickly, too quickly, and found that her head spun just a little. It was a feeling she didn't like, but it soon passed. She wiped her hands across her face to awaken the skin and cleanse the sleep from her eyes, suddenly remembering that she'd shot Cato last night. She shivered.

As she dressed for the day, she realized everything that had happened last night happened in such rapid succession that there was no time to think. The dog barking, her glimpse of the dark figure at the guest house door, the race down the stairs to act as backup for Ida, grabbing the shotgun when she found her asleep, making her way to the dark living room, even firing the gun seemed to all run together as one action triggered by some outside force. She had actually fired a shotgun, not just fired it, but fired it at another human. She had never fired a gun before and hoped she never would again. Then she remembered telling Ida that she'd done it for Junior. Why she'd said it, she wasn't quite sure. She recalled wondering if she'd gone too far, insisting Ida retract her offer for them to stay.

When she reached the kitchen, she found the sink lined in dirty glasses and coffee cups and recalled having insisted on making a fresh pot for the police. Ida had taken over when her hand was too shaky to measure the coffee without spreading grounds all over. She could smell the damp grounds left in the coffeemaker, knowing that Ida would have never thought to clean it out before going to bed. She filled the sink with warm water and soap and began the cleanup.

They would be leaving today, she thought as she swirled a soapy cup under the cold water tap to rinse it, after dinner, no doubt. And she found that thought a sad one. The house would return to its routine. Ida would be bored and moody at first but that would pass. They would... would what? What was it that had occupied their years of living alone in the house? She realized now how boring they had both become.

She dried her hands and reached for the coffee pot, filling it with water and measuring out the coffee grounds. At least her hand wasn't shaking today.

Ida pushed the swinging door open, walking sleepily to the sink without speaking, to add a cup she'd taken with her to bed. She yawned broadly, looking at Madeline's scowling face when she'd finished her stretch. "What's the matter?" she said.

"You know you're not to have coffee after seven.

Doctor Ross was very adamant on that."

Ida ignored her, making her way to the cupboard for a fresh coffee cup and saucer. "Feeling better this morning. I see," she said stopping at the coffeemaker. "No coffee yet?"

"Yes. Better. Not great but better."

"Good," Ida said, squeezing Madeline's thick arm. "I'm so proud of you. Took guts. Not sure I could have."

"We need to talk," Madeline said.

"Don't worry. They're leaving after dinner. Junior told me that he asked Dawkins to talk to their landlord. Explain what happened." Ida pulled out a chair to wait for the coffee to finish perking.

Madeline pulled out a chair next to her. "That's what we need to discuss." She searched the ceiling for a moment trying to find her next question. "What makes you think it could work?"

Ida was confused at first. Was it Dawkins' explanation to the landlord? Suddenly, she realized that Madeline was having second thoughts about their leaving. "You want them to stay then?"

"That's not what I asked. I asked. What makes you think it could work?"

The two old women locked eyes, reading each other as they often did. Ida's expression was blank at first as she struggled to gather her thoughts. She smiled slowly, saying, "I remember the day you came to this house. April and clear as a bell. You wore your blue-and-white polka dotted dress. Your shoes where low-heeled and bright white and you had on a white straw hat."

That dress again, Madeline thought. The dress, the hat, the shoes. Long gone, but they keep returning. Or was this some thought transference that two good friends share. It was less than a week ago that she had remembered them herself.

"We sat in the living room," Ida continued. "Just the two of us. And you told me you'd never been a domestic but that you could cook plain food and you would work hard. Do you remember that?"

"Yes."

"I hired you right then. Didn't even consult Jack. And Arthur took you to fetch your things. I never doubted you were the one," Ida said, leaning forward to pat Madeline's arm. "In the end you follow your instincts. I trusted them then and I trust them when it comes to Junior and Eula."

Madeline got up and went to get the coffee pot without saying anything. She returned to fill Ida's cup, saying, "We need to talk to Eula then."

~*~

The last thing Maria wanted to do was go to the parish children's pageant. She'd spent the last few days hovering by the phone, hoping they'd call to tell her she had the job. The interview had gone so well, she knew. And her placement officer had called her, after talking with the supervisor she'd met with, to tell her everything looked good. Expect a call, she'd said. But still no call. She wondered if she would hear if they decided to hire someone else. And here it was Friday and Christmas day, and she knew she wouldn't hear anything until Monday. No one would call her until Monday.

She washed her face and tied her thick black hair into a makeshift ponytail. Her reflection told how little sleep she'd had since losing her job, and she'd noticed that she no longer struggled with the button on the waist on her slacks. She sighed, thinking she was too tired to face a bus ride with the boys. She wondered if there wasn't something else that would satisfy them closer to home, but the boys were already pounding on the bathroom door, asking her to hurry up. So she gave in, opening the door and pretending she was excited, too.

Julio and Eduardo pulled at Maria's baggy pants as

they made their way through the unruly crowd of children and parents lining the street in front of *La Nuestra Senora De Los Angeles* church. Crowds always made her nervous when the boys were with her, knowing their habit of playing dodge 'em with each other. She'd warned them that if they got out of hand they wouldn't get to stay for the procession. They were to hold onto her hands until they were safely seated along the curb, but that had shifted to her khaki slacks shortly after leaving their apartment.

After two blocks with no luck, they found a small stretch of vacant curbing and settled in to wait for parade of children dressed to reenact the journey of the three wise men. And she instructed them that they were to fall in behind the procession along with the other children to walk in silence to the manger in the parking lot next to the church. Before long the curb filled to capacity with other children anxious for the parade to start.

The tinkling bell of an ice cream truck sent the boys into action, jumping up and down, yelling along with the other children surrounding them. "Ice cream! Ice cream! Ice cream!" they chanted in unison first and then in tandem as the truck pulled to a stop and prepared to work the crowd in advance of the parade. The other children ran to mob the truck while her two boys continued begging for permission to join them. Maria gave in, allowing them to race to the truck. She knew they'd waste the four quarters she'd put in the bottom of their Christmas stockings on overpriced cones, but it was Christmas and they were young.

She sat down on the curb to save enough space for her boys and began talking to one of the other Hispanic mothers nearby. She noticed that her English wasn't as good as Maria's and that seemed to make her feel better. She hoped that the other applicants the supervisor had interviewed lacked her fluency in English. She knew that all of her competition had been predominately Hispanic.

Before long, Eduardo ran to her side as she spoke with the woman, clamping his chubby little arms around her neck, sobbing uncontrollably. She took his arms in her hands and forcefully released his grip on her neck, half ignoring him, knowing he was easily upset and not wanting to encourage his behavior.

"Shush," she said softly. But when she looked at him, she saw this was not some small slight. "What is it, Eduardo?" she asked, holding him at a distance to scan his legs and arms for a scrape or some other cause for his distress.

Eduardo continued to sob as he reached both hands into his pockets, reversing them for his mother to see how empty they were.

"You lost your money? Is that it?"

But Eduardo could only sob, and so she reached over to pull him onto her lap and hugged him. "Don't cry, now," she said, lifting the strap of her purse from her shoulder and opening it to look for her coin purse.

As she dug around in the jumble of her purse, she saw Julio walking back from the truck eating a double-dipped ice cream cone and carrying a candy bar. She felt her face flushing as she realized what had happened. She lifted Eduardo from her lap and stood. "Come here!" she growled. "You come right over here!" Julio's eyes widened, knowing only too well the vein that stood out on his mother's forehead.

Maria looked down at Eduardo. "Did he cheat you out of your money? Did he?" She knew how cunning Julio could be.

"No," he said, shaking his innocent face, and he rubbed his wet eyes with his fists. "It was here last night," he said, touching his reversed pockets.

Maria whirled around, grabbing Julio so violently that the two dips of ice cream toppled from the cone onto the pavement, splattering onto Maria's shoes. "Madre de Dios!" she said, lapsing into the Spanish she never used with her boys, wanting them to speak perfect English. "You stole from your own brother!"

With that, she lifted her free hand and swatted Julio's butt. It was something she rarely did, but she was tired and greatly disappointed, and Julio immediately began to cry. She lifted her arm again but stopped, holding it high into the air, frozen by the image of the purse on her shelf.

Maria slowly released her grip on Julio and sank to the curb. The muffled sounds of her crying, something they had never seen her do, brought the boys to her side to touch her gently on the shoulders. She reached out and hugged them close to her, ignoring the stares of the crowd all about them.

CHAPTER THIRTY

Eula stopped to open the oven door an inch or two, inhaling deeply and admiring the golden-brown bird. The sweet potatoes had a matching caramelized glaze, and she smiled her approval. Junior stood behind her, holding the two gifts, one wrapped and one not, and looking impatient. It was to be their farewell to Ida and Madeline, Dawkins having coerced Mr. Raymond into letting them back into their apartment, and he preferred getting on with the unpleasant task of saying good-bye after dinner.

They found Madeline and Ida in the living room, Madeline's head resting against the back of the sofa, her eyes closed. Ida sat in the big winged-back chair and looked up from an old leather-bound book copy of *A Christmas Carol.* The lights of the Christmas tree were lit and reflected off the five or six presents in gaily colored wrapping and the shiny surface of the highly polished floor.

"Dinner sure smells good," Eula said and went to Ida for a hug.

Madeline woke up with a start and wiped at her tired eyes. "Hope you two are hungry."

"Junior's always hungry," Eula said, moving to her new friend and leaning down for another hug.

Junior handed Madeline the smaller of the two boxes. "Merry Christmas. Just a little something for all you've done for us," he said, leaning down for his hug, too. "From Gramma and me."

"You shouldn't have," she said, tearing into the paper and lifting the top of the box. She held it to her nose and took a noisy whiff of the three bars of scented soap. "Almost as good as my turkey."

Junior walked over to Ida, who stood watching Madeline lift the soaps one at a time. He held out the large flat box to her. "Merry Christmas," he said, giving her a kiss on the cheek. "Couldn't think what you'd want or need," he said as Ida took a seat. "It was the only thing I knew you didn't have."

Ida stared at the box, wondering if there hadn't been enough paper left to wrap them both. She lifted the lid, folding back the inner paper. "Shouldn't have spent—" she began, dropping the lid to the floor and lifting the blue cardigan from the box as furrows began to form between her eyebrows.

"Not cashmere. All we could afford," he said, noticing the furrows and matching them with his own.

Ida held the sweater to her breast, looking away, her eyes resting on the silver-framed photo of her son.

"Thought you should see it before wrapping it." He waited for a moment, expecting some kind of response. "He's not here yet. Is he?" But Ida said nothing. "Not the right size?" he asked, thinking something was terribly wrong here.

"It's... It's..." was all she could get out. She stood suddenly and left the room, the tapping of her heels on the staircase echoing in the hall.

Junior turned to see Madeline's head bowed slightly and shaking. "What is it? What did I do?"

Eula rose from her seat next to Madeline and walked

across the room, lifting the photograph.

"Nothing," Madeline said, softly.

"He's dead, isn't he?" Eula said, looking back at Madeline.

"Yes."

"Dead?" Junior said.

Eula tilted her head as she looked at Donald's smiling face in the photo. "Must've been in his twenties. I wondered why there were no current ones."

Madeline reclined against the back of the sofa. "When the telegram came, she refused to believe he was dead. Missing in action, it said... Have you ever seen a telegram?" she said, sitting back up and looking at Junior. "No, I don't suppose you have. Little strips of paper, the words typed out on little strips of paper, cut out and glued to it, and you wonder— Did they get the right ones? Are these the words for me? Anyway, they never did find him."

"Vietnam?" Eula asked.

"Yes. He was a doctor. He volunteered. I thought that eventually she'd come to accept it. Maybe one day."

"Why didn't she tell me?" Junior said, turning to look toward the hallway.

~*~

He saw the light bisecting the long hallway and followed the worn path in the Oriental carpet, stopping to look around the door frame. It was a boy's room, pennants and posters, deep blues and bright reds, the kind of room that would have been noisy and messy. It was neat now. It smelled like sandlewood soap or perhaps cedar. Junior watched her as she closed one dresser drawer and opened another, taking out the odd items only a boy could have collected.

Ida sensed someone was there. She didn't turn to see who it was, but she'd heard the creaking of the wooden floor muffled by the carpet. She closed the drawer and turned, expecting it to be Madeline come to pep-talk her into rejoining the group. She looked at Junior, seeing at first just his size, and found she was unable to speak.

"Why didn't you tell me?" Junior said, taking a step into the room, feeling awkward, one arm hanging useless, the other holding the blue cardigan.

Ida looked away. "I still can't say it out loud."

Junior drew closer, wishing there was something he could say, something that would help.

"Look here," Ida said, pulling the two doors of the closet open wide.

He stared into the darkness as Ida reached in to pull the string of the overhead light. The faint scent of moth balls greeted him as he stepped forward. On the floor beneath the neat row of shirts and sports coats, he saw them stacked five high, the stacks stretching the width of the closet. Each one was wrapped in gaily colored paper, twenty nine of them.

Ida stared at them. "There are things in life, things that you shouldn't have to accept... Times when you think God has forsaken you," she said in a voice he could barely hear.

Junior watched her staring into the closet and wondered how she had managed to avoid facing the truth for all these years.

"I met a lady on the bus once," he said, wondering if this was his business but unable to stop. "She told me God doesn't do those things."

Ida turned to look up at him. "She did?"

"Yes. And I wanted to believe her," he said, seeing the tears running down her pale cheeks.

"You did?"

"Yes. I did. I still do."

Ida brushed the tears from her cheeks and smiled. "Me, too."

Junior took her by the shoulders and hugged her close to him. When he pushed her back, he pulled a handkerchief from his pocket and handed it to her. Ida blotted at her cheeks and sniffled, offering another smile.

"I can tell you this much. He is awfully lucky to have a mother who loves him this much," he said, looking down into her eyes and smiling. He lifted the cardigan, opening it with both hands, and reached over the tiny woman, placing it on her shoulders. "I think this one is for you, now. Merry Christmas, Mrs. Hanson."

Ida reached up with one hand to feel the soft wool. "Merry Christmas, Mr. Thomas," she said, taking his arm and walking out the door.

~*~

Ida pushed the long sleeves of the blue cardigan up to her elbows, looking up from Eula's too-long grace, and lifted her water glass, appreciating its crystal heft. Her eyes scanned the table, thankful for more company than just Madeline's and knowing that she probably felt the same way.

"I'd like to propose a toast," she said, making sure that everyone had time to lift their glasses. "To Doctor Junior Thomas."

The three women leaned in to clink glasses as Junior set his down quickly on the table.

"What's that supposed to mean?" he said, looking unhappy.

"Now, Junior," Eula said, "just listen."

"The three of us had breakfast this morning while you slept," Ida said, taking over. "Sort of a meeting of the minds. Didn't we, ladies?" Eula and Madeline nodded. "You're going to school full time."

Junior twisted the water glass in small circles with his right hand without looking at the three women. Eula recognized his embarrassed resistance and hoped he'd just keep quiet.

"Is that right?" he said with a scowl.

"We need help around here," Ida continued. "I'm offering the apartment plus six hundred a month."

Madeline shot Ida a glance, indicating her disapproval. "Ahem," she added, further prodding her friend.

"Eight hundred a month."

Junior's eyes narrowed to slits. "We don't want charity."

"Junior!" Eula said, thinking he was being rude.

Madeline knocked her fist on the table to gain attention. "It's not charity," she said firmly.

"Charity you get from strangers," Ida said. "Friends like to think they're helping."

"Besides, it's a fair exchange. Lots to be done around this old house, and you can do most of it around your school schedule," Madeline said.

"With my Social Security, there'll be plenty to pay for whatever else you'll need," Eula said, giving Junior a *please-say-yes* look.

Junior looked down at his untouched plate of food. "You're forgetting one thing, aren't you?" he said, not looking up.

"Queen? I mean Mae." Ida corrected herself in deference to Eula, knowing how she hated the name. "No, we haven't forgotten her."

Junior looked at Ida, wondering if she actually knew how much trouble Queen could cause. "She's trouble. What if she comes back?"

"Maybe she'll make it? Maybe she won't? I know this much. We all have to face trouble. Have to..." Ida said, hesitating to glance at Madeline. "Learn to move forward and not sideways." Madeline smiled.

"But what if she does come back?" he said.

"That's a bridge we'll all cross together. For now, I hope, we all hope, you'll accept our offer."

"I... I couldn't," he said, avoiding the three sets of eyes.

"Nonsense!" Ida said, "We all need each other. Everyone needs someone to be proud of; we've elected you."

Eula could see he wasn't sold. "You have to learn to accept what people offer out of love, Junior."

He sat silently, rotating the sweaty water glass, overjoyed at the opportunity but not knowing how to say yes. He finally looked up and offered them a smile, lifting his glass.

"Doctor Junior Thomas," Ida said.

~*~

Madeline wiped the last tidbits of food from the counter and hung up her towel. She was tired but pleased with the way that her dinner had gone and strangely excited to know the house would be alive once again. She pushed open the door to the front hall, finding Ida standing by the table under the mirror holding the photograph of her son. Ida looked up at her and set it back on the table.

"Guess there are just some things that even God can't make right," Ida said.

Madeline put her arm around Ida's shoulder, patting it repeatedly. "Maybe sometimes he just puts a different face on things," she said.

Ida ran her hand over the arms of the cardigan sweater and smiled weakly. The doorbell rang, startling them.

~*~

The blast of fresh air was like a wakeup call as Ida stepped out onto the front porch, drawing up her arms to rub her elbows briskly with her hands. She caught sight of the Mexican woman scurrying down the sidewalk, headed in the direction of Wilshire Boulevard. She wondered if the doorbell had been some sort of prank. Thinking something was vaguely familiar about her, though, she stepped forward to get a better look as the woman passed under the street light.

Ida's foot hit it squarely, sending it sailing to the edge of the steps. She stepped to the side, allowing the porch light to find the purse. She looked back down the street, but the woman was gone. Stooping down, she lifted the purse and turned to open it under the light.

Ida did a quick inventory, seeing her one credit card, the sunglasses with the cracked lens, and her wallet. Unsnapping the wallet, she pulled out the wad of money, leafing through it, finding it was all there.

She smiled as she closed the purse and took another look down the street just in case. She turned and went into the house, closing the door behind her and shutting off the light.

The lace curtain in the window next to the door was drawn back and a small pale hand removed the *Guest House For Rent* sign.

THE END

AUTHOR'S BIO

To date, John has written two novels, five screenplays and short stories. The screenplay version of this novel is also available from this author.

John lives in Palm Springs, California where he writes screenplays and novels when not walking his dogs. He loves the desert air and near constant sunshine.

COMING SOON

Talking to Albert

A former showgirl battles with her control-freak niece to keep her home, driver license and avoid the dreaded "Old Folks Home." But she shoots herself in the foot by taking in the newly-released, and maybe not cured pyromaniac son, of an old friend who promptly falls in love with her Jewish/Hispanic cleaning lady with a history of gold digging.

There's hell, fire and brimstone in the Hollywood Hills when these quirky characters create a cross between "Sunset Boulevard" and "Harold & Maude."

CPSIA information can be obtained at www.ICGtesting.com
Printed in the USA
LVOW031458231111

256297LV00001B/51/P